I dedicate this book, to a    ʒ
help and practical suppo   ꞁave
remained a manusᵥ   ᵥwer.
My heartfelt thanᵣ   ᵧʋu all.

Al Wilkinson

James Wilkinson - Editor

Craig Wilkinson - Illustrator

1

The Beast of Pencarron

By Al Wilkinson

Chapter One

"Dartmoor! Dartmoor!" I almost shrieked. "Over Christmas. Have you gone mad?" We had just finished the evening meal when Mum tossed this 'hand grenade' in amongst us. I should explain at this point that Mum is a competition freak. If she sees a competition in a magazine or newspaper or even on a can of baked beans she has to enter. She has won a few prizes from time to time but never anything like this.

"A five star hotel on the edge of Dartmoor, wow!" This was my sister Fiona, Fiona's fourteen, two years older than me and a bit of pain sometimes. Most of the time come to that. But that's sisters for you.

"Come on now Ben" said Dad with a smile. "A few days at a top class hotel for the four of us. This is the best thing your Mum has ever won. You should be happy for her."

"Sorry Mum" I said a little shamefaced "I am glad that you've won, but we always spend Christmas at home. Look" I said waving my arm about as if they hadn't noticed. "Fee and I have put up all these decorations. It took us all yesterday afternoon to dress the tree. Look! It's beautiful."

"It will all be here when we get back" said Dad.

"But it won't be the same will it? It won't be Christmas" I howled.

"I'm sorry it's such short notice Ben" said Mum, soothingly. "But the letter seems to have got held up in the Christmas post. It only came this morning." She passed the letter across to me. There it was in black and white an invitation for Mrs Elizabeth Warton and up to three family members to spend four days at the 'Tregarron Arms Hotel' near Tavistock from December the twenty-second to the twenty-fifth, leaving on boxing day.

"It says here that this is the second prize. What was the first prize? Two weeks in Siberia?"

Mum laughed. "No love, it was a Caribbean Cruise"

"Pity you couldn't have got that. Then all we would have had to worry about was pirates instead of hordes of escaped prisoners."

"What are you prattling on about" said Fiona, with a sneer.

"I suppose you do know there's a prison full of dangerous lunatics on that moor?"

Dad chuckled. "I don't think we need to worry on that score, Ben, they are all safely behind bars and high stone walls."

"Huh!" I snorted. "They are always getting out. It's in the papers practically every week. Armed robbers, murderers, all sorts. Give me pirates every time."

As I scooped up the last spoonful of apple pie I gazed gloomily at the Christmas tree standing in the corner. It glowed like a beacon with it's fairy lights, glass balls, crackers and tinsel. Ever since I can remember Fiona and I have always dressed the tree. It's one of the few things that we do together without getting up each others noses. A week or so before Christmas get out the boxes of ornaments and greet them like old friends. Some of them are older than we are. Glass balls, glass trumpets, little wooden toys, tiny crackers and goodness knows what. Yeah, at Christmas my sister and I are a couple of tree freaks.

"It's not just escaped convicts we have to worry about" I muttered, darkly. "There are hundreds of miles of mist covered marshes. It's a wilderness."

"Good Lord Ben" chuckled Dad, the way you talk it sounds like a damp version of the Gobi Desert. It's only twenty miles across you know."

"I've heard some weird tales about Dartmoor" I said "Legends and stuff."

"What Legends?" Asked Fiona.

"Well the giant hound for a start."

"You mean the 'Hound of the Baskervilles'?" Asked Fiona.

"Yes that's the one".

"It's a story, dummy" Fiona, scoffed

"I know that". I was on shaky ground here.

"Alright then, who wrote it?"

"What's that matter?" I blustered. "I bet it's based on fact".

"You don't know, do you?"

"Alright you two, that's enough". Put in Mum.

"Anyway" I said darkly. "Don't say I didn't warn you."

"We won't" smiled Dad.

"How many dresses shall I pack?" Fiona asked Mum.

I jumped in before Mum had a chance to reply. "It's a holiday not a fashion parade. Isn't that right mum?"

"Well they will expect certain standards Ben. You'll need to pack a suit".

"A suit" I gasped. "Why do I need a suit?"

"So that you don't come down to meals looking like a 'run over tramp' like you do at home" Crowed Fiona, spitefully.

"Sorry Ben". Said Mum. "But since we can't leave you here all alone over Christmas, I'm afraid you will just have to grit your teeth, pack your suit and brave the terrors of Dartmoor with the rest of us". If only she'd known.

Chapter 2

"There's no such word"

"Of course there is" I said, Indignantly. "You just haven't discovered it yet. Dumb girl".

"Alright then, what's it mean?"

Fiona and I were playing scrabble, in the back of the car. This was two days later while we were speeding down the M5, towards Bristol and the West Country. I was saved by the bell or rather by Dad, who was driving.

"Why don't you two read or something? Every time you play scrabble you sound like a couple of alley cats, disputing territory".

It was mid afternoon on a dull December day when we left the motorway, just south of Exeter. That was when Dad had the bright idea of leaving the main road and taking a route across the moor.

"There is plenty of daylight left" he said, airily. "We might as well take a look at Dartmoor since we are here. I'll take the road through Two Bridges, according to the map it goes near the prison. Maybe we'll see some of the convicts going home for Christmas, over the wall".

"Ha. Ha. Ha." I said, sarcastically.

"Do you think this is wise, John?" Said Mum, anxiously. "It gets dark early at this time of year, you know."

"Don't worry, Love, we shall be at the hotel long before dark". Famous last words. We drove along some narrow country roads until we reached Mortenhampstead, where there were signs for Two Bridges and Princetown.

"There you are look" said Dad, triumphantly. "It's only twelve miles to Princetown. That's where the prison is". Those narrow roads had slowed us down though and already the light was beginning to fade, heralding the approach of night. Then suddenly we were into it. The mist was thin at first and kind of like stands of gauze.

"Uh oh" I muttered.

"It's okay" said dad, confidently. "We'll drive out of it soon, I'm sure".

But we didn't, the mist got thicker. It was more like cotton wool than gauze now and Dad had to slow down and switch on his lights. It was late afternoon now and what daylight was left began to fade rapidly. The car was down to a crawl now and far from driving out of the mist, it seemed to be getting worse. Fiona, sat hunched in the corner, staring morosely out of the window.

"This is all your fault." She snapped, turning to glare at me.

"How on earth do you make that out?"

"Ever since Mum told us about her win you have been nothing but a Jonah! Moaning about legends and giant hounds and misty marshes. You're a jinx you are" she sniffed. "I've read about people like you. On the old sailing ships they used to throw your sort overboard."

"Oh I see, we travel to a place that's famous for it's mists and when we run into one, it's down to me. Thanks a bundle".

"Cut it out you two." Snapped Mum. "Your Dad has enough to cope with, without you two squabbling in the back."

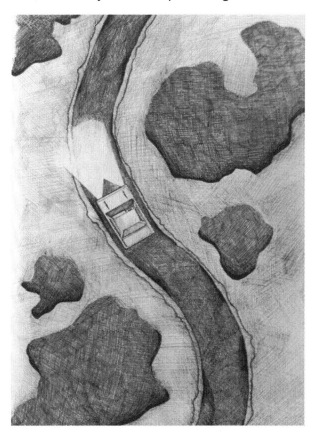

Chapter 3

Mum was right of course. It was quite dark now and the mist was thicker than ever and Dad was having trouble keeping to the road. After another hour of this Dad stopped the car and said, "I don't like this at all. I've got a horrible feeling that we are not on the right road, It's too narrow. The main road across the moor isn't exactly the M1 but it was wider than this.

"We just passed a post of some sort" I said, "It might have been a signpost. Shall I get out and take a look, Dad?"

"Alright son, here take this torch". He reached into the glove compartment and handed me this big silver torch. "And don't go out of sight of the car lights, okay?"

"Don't worry, I won't" I replied, stepping out into the mist. I gave a shudder at the cold embrace as the clinging tendrils wrapped themselves around me. It was like being touched by cold, dead fingers. I walked slowly back along the road, shining the torch and looking back longingly every few steps, at the car's lights. Suddenly there it was and thank goodness it was a signpost. I pointed the torch at the one finger board on the post and read the faded lettering, 'Boxwood 5 miles'. Just as I was about to turn and walk back to the car, the swirling mist parted, allowing light from the sickle moon above to briefly touch the moor. I stood rooted to the spot, unable to believe my eyes as through the mist, like players coming on stage, walked a string of pack ponies with barrels and boxes strapped to their backs. More un-nerving still was the fact that the men who walked beside them were dressed for another age. Some wore seaboots, their heads clad in bandanas. Others were garbed in long coats and 'tricorn hats' and all seemed to be wearing swords and pistols. They looked like a bunch of pirates. This couldn't be real. I must be seeing things. There wasn't time to feel fear for the mist closed like a curtain and they were gone. How long I would have stood there I don't know. I was already beginning to doubt the evidence of my own eyes, when there was a call from the car.

"Ben, are you alright?" It was Dad's voice. I shook my head, trying to rid myself of the feeling of unreality.

"Coming Dad" I called back, and trotted back towards the welcoming glow of the car's rear lights.

"Was it a signpost?" Asked Mum, as I climbed gratefully into the warmth of the car.

"Oh yes" I replied. "It was a signpost alright. But it didn't say anything about Two Bridges or Princetown, it just pointed to a place called 'Boxwood 5 miles'."

"Oh Lord!" groaned Dad. "I must have veered off the main road in this blasted mist. We'll just have to keep going and hope there's an inn or something in this Boxwood place. Otherwise we look like spending a cold night in the car, because I can't take much more of this". Dad started the engine and we began to crawl forward again.

"I saw something really weird while I was looking at the signpost" I began. They would probably think I was nuts but I couldn't keep it to myself, could I?

"What do you mean, weird?" asked Mum, turning in her seat.

"Well..." I hesitated, and Fiona jumped in.

"Don't tell us, you saw a Cornish Piskey sitting on top of the signpost." I glared at her.

"Be quiet Fee" said Mum. "Go on Ben"

"Well" I started again, "Just as I was about to start back, the mist kind of parted for a few seconds and I saw..."

"What, what?" Urged Fiona, impatiently. They weren't going to believe this, I wasn't sure I did now. Anyway, here goes, I thought. So I recounted just what I had seen and added, lamely, "I know it's hard to believe but that's what I saw."

"Oh my God!" drawled, Fiona, rolling her eyes like a drama queen. "Five and twenty ponies trotting through the dark. Dad, stop the car! We've got a loony on board." Then, sarcastically. "Who do you think you're kidding, little brother?"

"Is this another of your tall stories?" Said Dad, sternly. "We haven't forgotten the last one. The escaped panther, which turned out to be Mr Murchison's black German Shepherd".

"No, no, Dad, honest. I don't do that anymore. I saw them, I know I did."

"I suppose" Mused mum. "It's just possible that what Ben saw were people taking part in a village pageant or something".

"Mmm" said Dad, doubtfully. But Fiona, wasn't having that.
"In December, in the middle of Dartmoor, miles from
anywhere, in a thick mist? Come on mum, get real."
Then a shiver ran down my spine as a thought struck me.
Why hadn't there been any sound? A string of ponies and a
group of men walking within ten yards of me. There should
have been some sounds, even though they were walking
on grass. But I had heard nothing, not even a whisper. Only
a ghostly silence.

Chapter 4

We ploughed through the white clinging shroud Dad muttering under his breath and Mum. Leaning forward, peering anxiously through the windscreen. Fiona, and I, lolled silently in the back. Suddenly we shot up as Mum pointed to the left and said sharply. "John, what's that?" Dad, braked and we could just make out the vague outline of two stone pillars, to which were attatched sagging wrought iron gates.

"Saints be praised." Said Dad, with feeling. "It looks like the drive to a large country house". He turned the wheel and drove between the pillars, feeling his way carefully up the drive.

"Do you think we should?" asked Mum, nervously.

"Why not?" Dad, replied. "They can only tell us to get lost, though I doubt they will on a night like this." We didn't have far to go before we saw the lights. Dimly at first, and then looming out of the mist was a large old house which despite the lighted windows and coach lamps each side of the door, had a brooding sinister air about it. With it's black timbers, gables and turrets, the place looked as if it had been there since the beginning of time.

"Do you think that the Adam's family will mind us just dropping in like this?" I asked. Dad looked round, startled. "Who?"

"He's talking about that scary family on TV" said Mum. I think I'd sooner stay with the Adams family than spend anymore time in the mist". Said Fiona with a shiver. Dad pulled up in front of the main door and we all piled out.

"Good grief!" exclaimed Dad, "How lucky can you get. This place is an inn, look." He was pointing to a weather beaten sign above the door, which proclaimed 'The Lost Inn'.

"I'm not surprised it's lost, stuck out here." I said, with a shiver. Dad led the way up the three stone steps and pushed open the black studded door. We trooped in behind him and looked around curiously.

"I was right, it's the Adams place alright." I whispered.

"Be quiet!" Hissed Fiona.

We were in a large hall, lit by electric sconces set in the dark oak panelled walls. The place had a strange air about it, almost menacing. The floor was of large grey flagstones and at the end a wide staircase led into the gloom of the floor above. A door on the left bore the sign 'Bar' in olde worlde script and we all followed Dad, through it into a long low beamed room. A welcoming fire blazed cheerfully in the large stone fireplace and Mum, Fiona and I made straight for it while Dad went to the bar. As I glanced round I realised that the fire was the only cheerful or welcoming thing in the dimly lit room. The dozen or so men who occupied the room all seemed to be sitting in shadows and our sudden arrival obviously didn't fill them with joy. From the looks on the faces we could see, you would have thought we had just dropped in to rob the place.

"Cheerful bunch, aren't they?" Muttered Dad, as he came to the table. "I've ordered drinks, he's bringing them over." Dad didn't have to ask, he knew from long experience what we wanted. Gin and tonic for Mum, Cokes for us kids and a pint for himself.

"Evening" said the barman, grudgingly, as he placed the tray of drinks on the table. Dad, tried a smile as he thanked him. But it didn't work.

"Can you fix us up with rooms for the night?" He asked.

The barman rubbed his chin as he considered this. "Well sir, I don't know about that" he began.

"This is an inn?" said Dad, with quiet patience.

Well, yes of course Sir," he muttered. "But the thing is see we don't get many folk come to these parts this time of year. There's nothing ready if you see what I mean." He was looking real shifty now, his eyes sliding all over the place. Dad fixed him with the look he usually keeps for me when he knows I'm being economical with he truth.

"Lets put it this way. Either find us rooms or we shall be spending the night in your bar, because there's no way we're going out there again tonight".

"Come, come Tom, show a little hospitality. Mustn't make guests feel unwelcome." The man who stood by the table

seemed to have materialised out of thin air for none of us had noticed his presence until he spoke.

"Permit me to introduce myself. My name is Quentin Adams."

"I don't----Ow! Ow!" I was about to say 'I don't believe it' that ow, ow was caused by Fiona's foot hitting my shinbone. I find it amazing that a girl who is always bragging about her dainty feet can kick like a demented mule.

"Sorry" said Fiona, in a very unsorry tone. "I was just moving my leg". When I looked up Quentin Adams, was regarding me with eyes that sent a shiver down my spine.

"You were about to say something, young man?" he said coldly.

"Er, no sir, it was nothing." Then Dad, introduced us all and invited Adams to sit down and have a drink. He nodded gravely and ordered a whisky.

"I'm sure Tom will fix you up". Said Adams. "He's not a bad fellow. He's right though, not many visitors find their way here in winter. Will you be staying long?"

"No we are on our way to a hotel near Tavistock but we seemed to take a wrong turning in the mist, and here we are". Said Dad, ruefully.

"Mmm" said Adams, nodding sagely. "This moor is a rare old place for mists. None quite like it."

"How do you mean?" Asked Dad

"There's strange tales told of weird happenings when the mist blankets the moor." His cold eyes seemed to take some of the warmth from the fire.

"You can say that again." I said with feeling. Mr Adams, gave me that look again.

"Well I saw something" I said lamely.

"Oh for goodness sake." Groaned Fiona, "Don't spin that yarn about those ponies. Mr Adams will think that the mist has penetrated your brain."

"Ponies, what ponies?"

So I told him about our stop on the road just before we reached the inn and what I had seen. Or thought I'd seen, I was having doubts myself now.

"There's probably some simple explanation" chuckled Dad. But Quentin Adams didn't smile. Leaning back in his chair, he took a sip of whisky, his eyes still fixed on me.

"Oh there's an explanation alright" said Adams, softly. "But its far from simple". Though Quentin Adams was speaking to Dad, those penetrating eyes never left mine. I can tell you I didn't like that look one little bit.

Chapter 5

"As I'm sure you know, many years ago the Cornish coast was a famous haunt of smugglers. When the 'Gentleman' as they were known, had landed their contraband at some remote cove the goods were loaded onto pack ponies and moved inland. This they did as quickly as possible to avoid the customs officers who prowled the coast. But once on the moor there were many paths and trails they could take. The customs men could not watch them all and were being watched themselves. The 'Gentlemen' had many friends. On a moonlit December night in the year seventeen eighty six a string of ponies left Tremarrion Cove, heading for the moor. They were led by an infamous smuggler named Tom Pelham who somehow got wind of their pursuers, he led his men into the 'Great Pencarron Bog'. A terrible place covering over two hundred acres, that has claimed countless victims over the years. However they do say there is a safe path through the bog, known to a very few. Pelham was one of them. All would have been well, for the Customs men dared not follow them into that dangerous morass. Then it happened!"

"What did? What happened?" asked Fiona and I, almost together.

"Well, the mist seemed to come out of nowhere. Blotting out the moon and trapping men and ponies in the middle of the bog. The Customs Officers turned their mounts to head back. There was no way they were going to venture into the 'Great Pencarron Bog' mist or no mist. Then from the mist covered bog there came an awful sound. It was an obscene sucking noise followed by what could only be only be described as the frenzied croaking of a giant frog. The screams and shrieks that came from the bog that night were such as were never heard before by mortal man. Howls of anguish that seemed to freeze the very marrow in their bones. The Customs men were rooted to the spot with terror, but not for long. Despite the thick mist they wheeled their mounts round and spurred them into a gallop to escape those dreadful sounds. Then suddenly there was silence. Which in it's way was as terrible as the noises from the bog".

Quentin Adams sat staring into the fire for some minutes.

"Did they find them? The men and the ponies". Asked Mother, uneasily.

Adams shook his head slowly, without taking his eyes from the fire. "No they did not. Neither men nor ponies were ever seen again."

"Are you suggesting that what Ben thought he saw were the ghosts of these unfortunate men." said Dad.

Adams shrugged. "I'm not suggesting anything, but your son is not the only one to see the 'ghost ponies'. There have been many sightings over the years."

"But 'bog monsters' and ghosts" scoffed Dad. "I mean to say, who believes in such things nowadays?"

"Is there a monster in 'Loch Ness'? A 'Yeti'? A 'Big Foot'?" Adams spread his hands. "Who knows for sure? But one thing I do know. Things happen on Dartmoor, that defy any rational explanation. Those who mock them do so at their peril." Then with a murmured 'Goodnight' he was gone, leaving us feeling even more isolated and a little uneasy.

Just then a nervous looking woman, bustled in from behind the bar carrying a large tray, which she placed on the table before us. "Mr Adams, said you'd probably want some supper. So I heated up these pasties. They were only made this morning so they be nice and fresh."

The mouth watering aroma that came from the tray made everyone sit up and take notice. On the tray was a large dish of steaming, golden pasties, crusty bread and pale Cornish butter. This was accompanied by a bowl of green salad. Dad, thanked the woman, who told us to call her Molly, and ordered a bottle of wine and some soft drinks.

Mum shared out the pasties and we all tucked in to a much needed supper.

"Wow! These are wonderful. What are they?" I asked.

"Cornish pasties, dummy." Sneered my sister, in her superior tone. But I was too hungry to care.

"Well, they get my vote." I mumbled over a delicious mouthful.

"It's strange" said Dad, pouring the wine. "But they never seem to taste as good anywhere as they do in Cornwall." After our meal we all basked contentedly in the warmth of the fire while Mum and Dad finished their wine. When Molly came to collect the dishes, she asked, anxiously, "Was it alright for you?"

"It was more than alright" replied Dad. "They were the best Cornish pasties I've tasted for years."

"Nice of you to say so Sir" she smiled. "Tom will help you with your bags when you're ready. I've turned on the radiators, so they'll soon warm the rooms up. Mr Adams said you might like hot water bottles in the beds so mind you don't burn your feet when you get in." Then she bustled off.

To my surprise, as I glanced around, we were the only people left in the room.

"Everyone has gone but us" I remarked. "It's probably that perfume that Fee's wearing" Fiona just glared. Dad looked at his watch.

"Dare say they've gone to their beds. Which is where we had better be heading. I must say, I could do with some sleep after that drive."

I shivered as we stepped out into the mist to get our bags from the car. The silence was total. It was as if the moor was waiting and listening for something. I shivered again, but not from cold this time.

Chapter 6

With a case in each hand, Tom led us through the hall up the wide staircase and into the gloom of the upper floor. Taking some large keys from his pocket, he opened three doors. With his thatch of grey hair and bushy side whiskers, he reminded me of some medieval jailer housing newly arrived inmates. Mum saw Fiona into her room and then me into mine. The room was panelled in dark oak like the rest of the place and dimly lit by the wall lights which seemed to cast eerie shadows over the room. Just what I needed. "Someone should tell the management about hundred watt bulbs" I sniffed. Giving me a motherly peck on the cheek, Mum went to the door.

"Just get into bed love, you'll be asleep in two minutes knowing you. The light switch is over here by the door. Goodnight love, sleep tight." She closed the door.

Light switch! I'm in a strange old inn surrounded by mist in the middle of this ghost ridden moor, and I'm going to turn out the lights? No way Josè.

As I undressed I gazed around the room, apprehensively and wondered which of the panels slid noiselessly back, like in the movies. And that great wardrobe? Well they always had false backs, didn't they?

I scrambled quickly into the bed and pulled the covers up under my chin. But mum was right, in no time my eyes slammed shut and I was asleep.

I don't know what woke me but I sat bolt upright in bed, my heart going sixteen to the dozen. The lights were still on thank goodness, and nothing in the room seemed changed. But something was wrong, I could feel it. Then I heard it. Music. As if from a great distance. But not music exactly, not like I had ever heard. There was an organ playing and voices chanting and though it was faint, it was terrifying. The hairs on the back of my neck rose and I felt the chill of fear in my stomach.

Jumping from the bed I dashed for the door, flung it open and ran into the corridor and began knocking on Fiona's door. It was pitch black except for the feeble light from my open door. No reply. "Come on Fee" I muttered. I knocked again, louder this time. A frightened voice said, "Who is it? What do you want?"

"It's me Fee, please let me in!" After a moment the door opened and I rushed in.

"What in heavens name do you think you're doing?" The voice was not frightened now. "Banging on my door and barging into my room in the middle of the night. Have you gone mad Ben?"

"Never mind all that" I hissed. "Did you hear it?"

"Hear what? I was asleep until some idiot woke me up."

"The music. The awful discordant music."

"Music? Oh for goodness sake Ben, it was probably someones radio or TV. Go back to bed and let me get some sleep."

"Be quiet Fee, and listen please" My sister could see that I was upset and did as I asked and we stood there listening intently. But the old inn was wrapped in silence.

"I think you've had a nightmare Ben" said Fee, a little more patiently. "Come on back to bed with you now."

"No, I was awake. I know I was." I protested. "Look Fee, come to my room and listen. If you can't hear anything I'll go back to bed. Please Fee"

"Oh very well, if it will make you happy." She sighed. We went next door to my room and stood in the middle of the floor. Ears strained to catch the sound of the eerie music. Fiona started slowly shaking her head and was about to speak but I held up my hand to silence her. Then I saw her eyes widen. I knew she could hear it. So could I. Drifting as though carried on the wind.

"You hear it Fee? She nodded, still listening.

"I suppose it could be a TV or radio" She muttered, doubtfully.

"But it's not like music, it's... It's unearthly."

"Where do you think it's coming from?" I asked.

"I've no idea. But it's awfully scary." She gave a quick shudder. "Perhaps we should wake Mum and Dad?"

"Oh no. No way. They still don't believe me about those ponies. I've got a torch in my bag. Let's just go along the corridor and see if we track it down ourselves."

"Well alright." Said Fee reluctantly. "But not far and if we can't find it, it's back to bed. Okay?"

There were two small pools of light from our open doors but further along the corridor it was black as coal. I quickly switched on my torch.

"Which way?" I whispered.

"It doesn't matter. Go left." Hissed Fiona. "And keep quiet."

We tiptoed along, the torch beam lighting the way, straining our ears for the sound of that dissonant, creepy music. After about ten yards the corridor ended at a window. Heavy curtains closed against the winter cold. I parted the curtains and we peered out at the night. The dense mist still clung to the old building. Drifting and swirling, as if trying to find a way in. Fiona tugged her dressing gown more tightly around her and gave a shiver. "I've had enough of this. For pete's sake Ben, let's get back to our beds."

"Okay, I suppose you're... What's that? I thought I saw something."

"What's what? Oh my God!" gasped Fiona. "Ben, look.

Just as it had when I saw the ghost ponies, the swirling mist parted for a brief moment. A patch of ground was illuminated by starlight for no more than a second. But we both saw it. A stage coach with four horses in front, pawing at the ground. But no driver up on the box, and no passengers either. Then it was gone. Swallowed by the mist once more. We looked at each other in astonishment, the music quite forgotten.

"What on earth is a stagecoach doing down there Fee?" It wasn't exactly a question. My sister was frowning and slowly shaking her head. "It was gone so quickly. Perhaps it was some trick of the mist."

"Come on Fee, get real you saw it as plain as I did. It was there." My sister gave a shiver.

"There's something odd about this place. I'm going back to my room."

Chapter 7

We hurried back down the dark corridor towards the dim haven of light thrown by the open doors of our rooms. We were soon in our beds, with the room doors locked against, we knew not what. But despite the fears of the night I was soon asleep. The next thing I was aware of was Mum knocking on my door to call me for breakfast. Quite like home really. At breakfast, Dad informed us that the mist was as bad as ever.

"It seems that we are stuck here until it lifts. So we must try to make the best of it." He said with a shrug.

After we had eaten, Mum and Dad settled down to read in a small sitting room in which Molly had lit a fire. Fiona and I wandered around the old inn for want of anything better to do. We passed one or two of the other guests but apart from a muttered greeting they didn't seem inclined to be friendly. In the bar we came across Molly laying the fire.

"Good morning Molly" we chorused. She looked up and smiled.

"Morning both. It don't look any too good out there, do it?"

"No it doesn't" replied Fiona, politely.

"Did you sleep well?" asked Molly, placing dry sticks on the crumpled newspaper.

Fiona and I looked at each other. "Oh yes, thank you" I replied.

"We were just having a look round" Said Fee.

"Yes, 'tis a rare old place this. Been here for hundreds of years it has. Used to be a famous staging inn so they do say."

"For stagecoaches, you mean?" I asked.

"Of course. They all used to stop here."

"It's funny you should say that. About stagecoaches, I mean. Because we saw one last night. Didn't we Fee? Out in front of the inn, it was."

"It might have been some trick of the mist though." Said Fiona, Hurriedly. Molly stopped what she was doing and became quite still. Kneeling there with the sticks in her hands. She looked up at me with a strange expression on her face.

"What was it like, this coach?" She asked, hoarsely.

"Well we only saw it for a second." I replied. "But there didn't seem to be anyone on board. Just four horses in front."

"Oh my good Lord!" Exclaimed Molly, dropping the sticks and rising slowly to her feet. "You saw the Death Coach." Fiona and I looked at each other in alarm.

"Well we are not exactly sure, you know." Said Fiona, quickly.

"I jolly well am." I said, stoutly. "Like I said, it was only for a second. But I saw it alright. And so did you Fee."

"Why did you call it the 'death coach'?" Asked Fiona, wide eyed.

"Because misfortune always follows a sighting." Said Molly, darkly. "Tis a terrible bad omen and no mistake."

"But why an empty coach?" I persisted.

"Twas a terrible happening and very long ago. Not a fit story for young ears. Just forget about it." Molly turned back to her task.

"Oh come on Molly." I cried. "We are not exactly toddlers, you know. We did see the coach after all. I think we ought to know the story. Please Molly."

She hesitated. "Well alright, but don't blame me if neither of you can sleep tonight." Molly sat down at a nearby table and Fiona and I joined her.

"It was the terrible winter of seventeen eighty. Worst ever known in these parts and the Exeter to Plymouth coach had stopped at the 'Black Bull' in Two Bridges, for lunch and for the passengers to stretch their legs and get warm. They were bound for 'The Golden Hind' in Plymouth and were due to stop here to pick up mail and any passengers wanting to board. There had been snow on the ground for some days and the sky was still full of it. Snow began to fall before the coach left the inn and there was talk of delaying departure. However, the snow was light and the road across the moor open so they set off. After all, it weren't far to the inn here. But the snow began in earnest and a bitterly cold wind sprang up whipping the snow into a blizzard, which soon started clogging the road. Though the horses were fresh they were soon having difficulty trying to drag the heavily laden coach through the deepening drifts. The blizzard finally blew itself out and it stopped snowing. Then came the freeze. It grew colder than anyone had ever known it. The people at the inn here, stoked up the fired and waited for the arrival of the coach. But they waited in vain. It was a week before they found the coach. The horses were standing like statues, still harnessed. They'd frozen to death where they stood, poor beasts."

"Oh! How terrible" gasped Fiona.

"But what about the driver and the passengers?" I asked fearful of the reply, Molly shook her head slowly.

"There was no driver nor no passengers neither. And they was never seen or heard of again."

"But when the snow melted they must have found their... Well you know." Fiona, swallowed hard and her words tailed off.

"Their bodies?" Molly shook her head, firmly. "No miss, they never found hide nor hair of those sixteen poor souls from that day to this."

Chapter 8

In a small private sitting room, tucked away at the back of the inn, another and far different conversation was taking place. Though on the same subject.

"I heard it clear as day, Quentin. I was just passing the door of the bar, which was standing ajar, when I heard voices. It was those two kids. They were telling Molly, that they had seen a coach standing in front of the inn. Said they saw it from window during the night."

Quentin Adams sat bolt upright in his chair. "Are you sure?"

"Of course I'm sure. I heard them tell her about an empty coach with four horses and no driver. That's not something they could make up, is it? It was the 'Death Coach' sure enough."

"They saw it last night, you say?"

"Yes, though God knows what they were up to, wandering about in the middle of the night."

Quentin Adams, stared at the thin, bearded man who stood before him. But his mind was elsewhere.

"You know what this means, Victor?" Victor Edelman shook his head.

"They are both 'fey'. Don't you see. I knew the boy was. He saw the ponies, and only the true 'fey' are able to see through the veil of time. As well you know." Quentin Adams, rose from his chair and began to pace about the small room. His eyes were alight with an almost religious fervour. "Fey siblings" He muttered. "Delivered right into our hands." He stopped in front of the other man, as if coming to a decision. "We must have them for the 'raising'. They will be perfect Victor, and we may never have such a chance again."

"Kidnap them!" Exclaimed Victor Edelman, a startled look on his face. "Oh come on, Quentin, the 'raising' is not for two days yet. If those kids go missing the police will be all over this place, like a rash. Remember, we have had some close calls in connection with the other disappearances. Especially that girl from Boxwood"

"Yes, yes Victor, but they have never traced anything back to the inn here. So relax." Quentin Adams continued his pacing, stroking his chin thoughtfully.

"This opportunity is too good to pass up. We must bring the 'raising' forward."

"But we can't do that, man. The days for attempting the 'raising' are set down in the 'Book'. You know that."

"I'm well aware of that Victor, but there is a margin of three days each side of the dark of the moon. Is that not so?"

"Yes you are right but…"

"No buts, Victor. We will attempt the 'raising' tonight."

"Tonight!" Exclaimed, Edelman. "But that will mean a full meeting of the 'Brotherhood'."

"Of course, but that is no problem. They are all here at the inn anyway, ready for the 'raising'. Go and summon them, Victor. We meet at the temple in one hour. Quickly now, there is no time to lose."

Chapter 9

Wide eyed with excitement, we thanked Molly for the story and hurried to the sitting room where Mum and Dad were reading. We told them about our seeing 'The Death Coach' and went on to relate Molly's story to them. As we told our tale they were becoming more and more sceptical. Mum was doing her best not to smile and not making a very good job of it. Dad, pursed his lips and began to examine the ceiling. The way he does when listening to one of my brilliant excuses for some mishap or other.

"We are used to Ben's tall stories of course." said Dad with heavy sarcasm. "But now he seems to have got you hooked as well Fee."

"Well, it was just a glimpse." Said Fiona, weakening. Dad grinned.

"You mean that your brother put the idea into your head and you thought you saw something. That's more like it." Then his grin changed to a frown. "Anyway, what on earth were you two up to, wandering around in the middle of the night?"

"Oh we thought we heard something." I put in, quickly. "But it was nothing." There was no way I was going to mention the music now.

"Come on Fee." I said. "Let's find something to do."

When we had left the room, I turned to my sister. "Thanks for your support, I don't think." I snorted.

"I really am not sure I saw it, you know, Ben. It could have been some sort of trick of the light."

"Rubbish" I replied. "It was there alright. Or rather it wasn't if you see what I mean."

We mooched around the old inn for a while longer and Fiona gave a sigh.

"Some holiday this is turning out to be. I'm fed up."

"I know what" I said, getting one of my brilliant ideas. "Let's get our coats and go outside."

"Are you completely mad? Half a dozen steps and we'd be lost in the mist and probably wander into that bog." She gave a theatrical shudder. Fee's very good at theatrical shudders.

"No, we won't get lost. Trust me. We'll just walk around the inn. If we keep it in sight we can't get lost, can we? It beats hanging around round here, right?"

"Well, alright then. But not far, okay."

We hurried to our rooms and collected our coats, scarves, gloves and wooly hats. We let ourselves out of the front door. Feeling a bit like intrepid explorers braving the Arctic tundra. The swirling mist seemed to reach out as if trying to caress us with it's clammy fingers. Fiona shivered.

"Remember now, we are not going far." Turning up our collars we walked along the front of the old inn. At the end of the building we came to a wrought iron gate leading on to a gravel path. The gate stood invitingly open. As if beckoning us to follow the tree lined path, farther into the mist. I hesitated at the gate and felt Fiona's hand on my arm.

"No." She said, firmly.

"What do you mean, no?"

"I mean we are not going through that gate. Just round the inn, you said. Keeping it in sight, you said."

"Yes I know but this is a wide gravel path. If we stay on it we simply follow it the back the way we came. Beats walking round in circles don't you think?"

"Well, alright." Replied Fiona, doubtfully. "But not far. Okay."

We set off down the path, our feet crunching on the coarse gravel. The big, old trees bordering the path looked eerie with the swirling mist clinging to their dripping branches like wraiths. We walked on into the mist, my sister casting nervous glances on either side and muttering darkly all the while. She can be a real pain at times. But that's girls for you.

"I don't like this at all" she moaned. "Supposing we walk into a bog."

"For Pete's sake Fee! They are hardly likely to put a tree lined gravel path across a bog, are they?"

"No, I suppose not but... What's that?"

"It's only another gate." I replied, peering into the mist. "Stop being so jumpy, will you?" However, this gate did have a kind of roof thing over it. Once again the gate stood open and we passed beneath the roof, still following the path.

"Wonder why they want to put a roof over a gate?" I mused. At that point, Fiona stopped dead.

"I know what that is. It's a 'lych gate'." She cried.

"What's a 'lych gate'?"

"It's a gate that leads up to a church. It's where they bring out the bodies. Thanks a lot little brother, you've brought us into a graveyard. You idiot!"

She was right. Peering into the mist I could just make out the sinister shapes of the gravestones. Crumbling crosses, flat ones tilting drunkly as if the weight of centuries had finally been too much. Some were surmounted by stone angels which seemed to be staring down at us like birds of prey.

I stopped to peer closely at one of the headstones. It was dated seventeen hundred and something and belonged to a Septimus someone or other.

"What are you doing now?" Snapped Fiona.

"Just trying to make out the name on this gravestone. I think it says Count somebody. Name begins with a D. Then there's an R and an A. I think the next letter is a C. Good Lord!" I gasped, starting back as if in terror. "It spells 'Dracula'.

Fiona shrieked loud enough to wake the residents.

"It was a joke, a joke." I cried, hastily. "Calm down will you."

"You pig. You absolute pig!" Yelled Fiona, stamping her foot. "That settles it. We're going back to the inn, right now."

Turning furiously on her heel, she took a step forward and fell with a cry of pain. "Oh Lord! My ankle!" She moaned. I dashed forward and helped my sister to her feet. But she almost fell again. "It's no use" she gasped. "I can't put my weight on it." I sat her down on a headstone that had conveniently fallen flat. The fellow who it belonged to had been dead for two hundred years, so I don't suppose he cared much. Fiona started to pull off her boot, until I stopped her.

"Leave it on Fee." I said. "If it's a sprain and it swells you'll never get it back on again." I don't know where I picked up that bit of knowledge.

"It's not much use to me if I can't walk, is it?" She snapped.

"It is if you don't want your foot to freeze. I remember reading about this chap in Alaska who..."

"Never mind your chap in Alaska, I'm starting to freeze." Wailed Fiona. I looked round desperately. Fiona was right. This icy mist seemed to creep into your bones. Then I had one of my bright ideas.

"Look, Fee. If they've got a graveyard and a lych gate, it stands to reason there must be a church nearby, right?"

"So what?" moaned poor Fiona, grimacing with pain. "I can't walk to it, can I?"

"Sure you can if I support you. Just put your arm around my neck." I helped my sister to her feet. "See, I can take your weight." Putting my arm around her waist we began to hobble slowly along the path.

Chapter 10

We made painful progress. Painful for Fiona, that is. She
was oohing and aahing, every step we took.

"Hold on Sis. I think I can see something up ahead." Sure
enough, through the mist loomed the vague outline of a
large stone building. But my sigh of relief was suddenly
stifled as something else swam into view.

"Good grief! What's that?" I exclaimed. Fiona lifted her head
and drew in her breath, sharply.

"Oh Lord! Not more ghosts?" She pressed closer to me.
The cause of our consternation was the procession of black
cowled figures emerging from the swirling mist and heading
in the direction of the gloomy grey stone building which we
could now just discern as the Norman tower of an old
church. They made no sound as wraith like, the column
seemed to float towards the church. Through the great
arched doorway they filed and as the last figure
disappeared into the dark interior there was a very
unghostly thud of a door closing.

"There! Did you hear that?" I cried, eagerly. "They're flesh
and blood alright. Ghosts don't open and close doors. They
float right through them. Right?"

"Yes, I suppose so." Replied Fiona, grudgingly. "But it all seems a bit weird though."

"Weird or not, if they are monks, they might help us get back to the inn. After all, that's what monks do, isn't it? Help people. Come on Sis, they can only say no."

Half carrying Fiona, we finally reached the church. The gloom beneath the arched porch was like the entrance to a cave as Fiona leaned, stork like against the ancient stones. Gripping the wrought iron ring, I pushed on the heavy oak door. Silently, it swung open. I thought they were supposed to creak. They always do in the movies.

Going back to Fiona, I put my arm around her and we were soon surrounded by the cavernous gloom of the old church. "It's awfully dark in here" Whispered Fiona, nervously. She was right. With all these monks who had just arrived, I had expected some light. Candles or something. Sitting my sister down on one of the pews, I gazed around. My eyes now becoming adjusted to the gloom.

"I don't believe it." I muttered. "The place is empty."

"It can't be. We just saw about two dozen people go in." Said Fiona, in a whisper. I don't know why we were whispering, but folks do that in church. It's as if they are afraid of disturbing God.

"That's if they were people." Added Fiona, ominously.

"Of course they were." I said, though without much conviction.

"They probably went out of another door."

"Why would they do that?" Hissed Fiona. "They only just came in here."

"How do I know for Pete's sake. Look, I'll go and take a look down at the far end."

"And leave me here on my own." Squeaked Fiona. "Don't you dare."

"Oh for goodness sake Fee, I won't be far away. This isn't a cathedral, you know."

"Alright, but don't go out of my sight."

"Okay, okay." I muttered and began walking slowly to the far end of the church to where the altar should have been. Only this place didn't seem to have one. Strange that. I was getting a prickly feeling in the back of my neck. For although there was a small door at the back here, the monks couldn't have left through it. There were old pews and goodness knows what piled up against it. It looked as if it hadn't been used for years. In fact the whole place had a sad neglected air about it.

Where on earth had they all gone? Fee's voice echoed hollowly.

"What are you doing Ben? Come back here, I'm scared."
She wasn't the only one. Going back to where she was
sitting I told her about the door.

"You obviously didn't look properly." She snapped. "We saw
them come in, didn't we? They must have gone
somewhere. People don't just dissapear into thin air." We
looked at one another and Fiona gave me a shudder. "Let's
get out of here. There's something not right about this
place. It's giving me the creeps."

"What about your ankle?"

"It's beginning to feel a little better. I don't think it's sprained
after all. Just give me a hand, will you?" Fiona tested her
weight on the ankle and after a couple of steps found that
she could walk on it, albeit with a limp. We were both glad
to leave the church, which had now taken on an air of
menace.

Chapter 11

We followed the path back the way we had come. The inn was a welcome sight as it loomed up from the mist. It was doubly welcome for it meant security and warmth. The incident at the church had left us both feeling unnerved and by now, despite coats, hats and gloves we were chilled to the bone. There was no one in the bar but the fire blazed like a beacon. We huddled round the old stone fireplace, letting the glorious warmth seep into us.

"Ooh that feels wonderful." Cooed Fiona.

"It sure does" I agreed.

"Shall we tell Mum and Dad about the church and the disappearing monks?" Asked Fiona.

"Are you crazy? One more story from me about anything that smacks of the supernatural and Dad will blow his top. I think he is already considering putting my name forward for the next 'village idiot' when there is a vacancy."

"But I saw them too, I'll back you up."

"Oh yes! Like you did about the 'Ghost Coach'. I don't think so."

My sister had the good grace to blush. Then I had a bright idea, which in the fullness of time we both came to regret, bitterly. "I tell you what!" I exclaimed, snapping my fingers. "Let's ask Molly, she seems to know everything about this place." As if on cue, at that moment, Molly, herself passed the door, carrying a mop and bucket. I called out to her and she stopped and stood in the doorway smiling, inquiringly.

"I thought I saw you two go out a while back."

"We just went out for a walk" I said.

Molly, frowned and shook her head. "You take care now. It's not a good idea going wandering about in this mist. We don't want you ending up in the great bog. Do we?"

"Oh, we didn't stray from the path." I reassured her. "We walked down to that old church and Fee went and twisted her ankle. Didn't you sis?" Fiona nodded and said. "We saw some monks go into the church. All in black they were."

Molly turned pale. "Monks? What nonsense. You couldn't have. There be no monks round these parts. Probably some trick of the mist. Anyway, that be a bad place. No one don't go near it. Nor should you neither." She bustled off, muttering to herself. Fiona and I, looked at each other, questioningly.

"That didn't go down very well, did it?"

"No." Mused Fiona. "Do you think it could have been... You know, just shadows?"

"Oh yes." I scoffed. "Shadows that bang church doors. I don't think so. What's the matter Fee, don't you trust your own eyes anymore? You saw them clear enough."

"Yes, you're right Ben. They were real alright. Molly's right about one thing though. There is something scary about that church."

I nodded in agreement. "And it didn't have an altar. Odd, wouldn't you say?"

Chapter 12

As we left the bar we ran into Mum and Dad.

"Hello, you two." Smiled Dad. "Where have you been this morning? Ghost hunting again?" He chuckled at his own joke and Mum smiled.

"Your Mum and I are just going for a drink before lunch. Are you going to join us?" We both nodded and followed Mum and Dad back into the bar. Come to think of it, I was feeling jolly hungry myself. Dad rang a small hand bell and Tom, appeared behind the bar, looking decidedly edgy. Ordering drinks, Dad led the way over to a table near the fire and Tom brought them over to us.

"Don't look like you folks will be leaving today." He said, glumly. "Mist be thicker than ever."

"Never mind" said Dad, stretching his legs towards the blazing hearth. "We are not exactly suffering, are we? Things could be a lot worse. In fact, I'm getting to quite like this place."

"Glad to hear it Sir." Muttered Tom. Though he sure didn't sound glad. As he walked away, he said "Lunch will be ready in about half an hour. If that's alright?"

"Thank you." Said Mum. "That will be perfect."

"Anyway, what have you been up to this morning?" Asked Dad.

"Oh, we just went for a walk." I replied.

"What! In all the mist." Mum exclaimed. "I hope you went well wrapped up."

"Oh Mum, of course we did. Don't fuss. We are not children you know." Said Fiona, loftily.

"We found a weird old church and graveyard." I said, proudly.

"Oh, and Fee twisted her ankle."

"Are you alright, love?" said Mum, concerned. "Let me have a look." With a sigh, Fiona lifted an ankle and Mum felt around it gently. "It doesn't seem to be swollen."

"It's okay now Mum, honest. I can hardly feel it." My sister gave me one of her withering glances. "It wouldn't have happened at all if your idiot son hadn't said he found Dracula's tombstone."

"Oh Ben!" Mum exclaimed.

"It was a joke, a joke." Dad, smiled despite himself.

The dining room, when we entered, seemed a little bleak, in spite of the blazing fire. Probably because we were the only guests in sight. Dad looked around and then glanced at his watch.

"Where is everyone? It's one fifteen."

"Perhaps the bog monster's got them." I said, rolling my eyes and making claws with my fingers, while gurgling horribly.

"Tell him to stop it Mum." Cried Fiona.

"Yes that's quite enough, Ben." Snapped Dad.

"I wouldn't mind feeding you to a bog monster." Muttered Fiona.

"Cut it out, the pair of you." Said Mum, sternly.

Molly, who served lunch, was rather subdued.

"Where is everybody?" Asked Dad, gesturing at the empty room.

"I really couldn't say Sir." Mumbled Molly, scuttling back to the kitchen.

Dad shrugged. "Odd." After finishing our lunch we rose to leave. Still no one had come into the dining room. "Very odd." Mused Dad as we left and strolled into the hall.

"Your Dad and I are going into the lounge for coffee." Said Mum. "And I don't want you leaving the inn again in this mist. Do you hear?" We both nodded. "How is your ankle Fee?"

"Oh, it's alright now Mum, honest." Replied Fiona, flexing her foot a couple of times.

"Good, because I think they have a games room upstairs and they may have Table Tennis."

"Oh great!" Exclaimed Fiona, brightening up. "Come brother, follow me to the thrashing of your life."

"That'll be the day." I scoffed. Mind you I have to admit that Fiona was a pretty fair player. For a girl, that is.

"Anyway they probably won't have any bats, and if they do there won't be a ball in the place."

"Don't be such a misery." Said Fee, heading towards the staircase.

Sure enough, when we found the games room, there was a table and bats but no ball. "Oh great!" Snorted Fiona.

"Told you so." I shrugged. "It never fails."

"Well at least let's go down and ask Molly. If anyone in this place knows where there's a Table Tennis ball, it will be Molly."

As we left the games room, we ran smack into Tom, who seemed to have been lurking in the passage outside. He started, guiltily and I don't know why but I got a strange, uneasy feeling that he had been following us.

Chapter 13

"Hi, Tom" said Fiona. "We need a Table Tennis ball. Any idea where we can find one?"

"Don't rightly know Miss." He replied, rubbing his hand over a whiskery chin, his eyes shifting all over the place. Then a sly look came over his face.

"Maybe I do though. But I ain't promising, mind."

"Oh good." chirped Fiona, eagerly. "Where?"

"I think there might be some in the cellar."

Fee and I looked at each other, with raised eyebrows.

"Why would there be Table Tennis balls in the cellar?" I asked, curiously.

"I ain't saying as there are for certain." Said Tom, huffily. "But we keeps lots of things down there. Do you want to come and look or not? 'Cos I've got work to do."

"Yes of course." I said, hastily. "Come on Fee."

"Right, we'll go down the back stairs, it'll be quicker."

I don't know why, but I felt vaguely uneasy as we followed Tom down the narrow back stairs. The cellar door was situated at the foot of a short flight of stone steps, the centres of which had been worn hollow by centuries of feet. Reaching up, Tom took a large iron key from a ledge above the door and turned it in the lock. He pushed the heavy, old door open (this one did creak).

"Hold on while I switch the light on." He said, reaching along the wall. A dusty bulb illuminated the steps, but only just. Reluctantly, Fiona and I followed Tom, down into the darkness below. He switched on another light at the bottom of the steps, which didn't do a whole lot to penetrate the sinister gloom in the far corners of the great vaulted cellar.

"I tell you what." Said Tom, as if the thought had just struck him. "While we're down here, would you like me to show you the secret passage?"

"Secret passage?" I said warily.

"Oh yes." Said Tom, rubbing his hands together, and managing to look like a sly miser. "Lots of these old places have them. This one comes out in the crypt of the old church. It was built so's the priests could escape if there was danger. That was hundreds of years ago of course. We don't normally mention it to guests, 'cos well, we can't have em' trampling about down here, see." He shrugged. "But as you"re down here you might as well have a peek." I looked at Fee.

"I don't like tunnels of any sort." She said, firmly. I must admit that I wasn't all that keen on the idea myself. But curiosity was getting the better of me. After all, I'd never seen a genuine secret passage. They were things I had only read about in adventure books. "I ain't suggesting you go along the tunnel. Not by no means. I couldn't allow that. But you can just step inside if you like. Be something to tell your friends about when you gets home, eh."

That did it. The thought of boasting to Mum and Dad, let alone friends, was irresistible. At least they couldn't accuse us of making this up. We would have Tom to back us up. "Come on Fee." I urged. "Can't you just see Mum and Dad's face when we tell them we've seen a real secret piece of history."

"Oh, alright, I'll have a look. But no way am I going in, okay."

"It's over in the far wall." Said Tom, leading the way past dusty wine racks, barrels of beer and crates of bottles. The cellar ended in a formidable stone wall.

"There it is." Said Tom, with a mocking grin on his face, gesturing towards the wall. "Just see if you can find the door."

Approaching the wall, Fiona and I, began peering at the stones for any signs of an opening. The rugged stones looked as solid and immovable as when the long dead hands of the masons had set them, centuries before.

"I can't see anything." Said Fiona, petulantly.

"That's 'cos you ain't supposed to." Tom chuckled. "Wouldn't be much of a secret if it was easy to spot, would it?"

"Well, how do you get in?" Asked Fiona, intrigued now, despite her dislike of tunnels.

"I'm just a'going to show you, missy." Replied Tom, reaching up to an old, rusty ring set in the wall. Twisting the ring to the right, he gave it a sharp tug. To our amazement there was a grating sound and a section of the wall swung slowly outwards, revealing the black mouth of a tunnel.

"Wow!" I exclaimed. "Is that clever or what. Look Fee."

"I am looking." Said Fiona, dubiously. "And clever or not, I'm not going in there. You can forget it."

"Well, I'm certainly going to take a look inside." I said, sounding a lot more like Indiana Jones than I actually felt. I still couldn't shake off the prickly feeling that there was some sort of menace hovering near. But there was no way I could back out now, was there? I would never hear the end of it. If I didn't at least step inside that tunnel, Fiona would use it as a stick to beat me with for ever more. Taking two steps into the tunnel, I turned to look back at the faces of Fiona and Tom, peering in from the cellar. There was a cold, clammy feel inside the tunnel. It was like putting on a wet coat. Taking a step back towards the entrance, I called to Fiona.

"Come on in Fee, the water's fine." She simply folded her arms, her lips set in a straight line. "At least put your foot inside so that you can say that you have been in a secret passage."

Fiona stepped closer to the entrance and peered fearfully in. "This is as close as I'm, ahhh!" At that point my sister dived headfirst into the tunnel; butting me in the midriff and knocking the wind out of me. She gave a terrified yell as we both crashed to the floor in a tangle of arms and legs. Before we could get to our feet, there was an ominous grating sound, followed by a thud, and then total darkness.

Chapter 14

When we finally sorted ourselves out, Fiona was clinging to me, gasping. "What on earth happened?"

"I don't know, you came in like a missile."

"I should think so, I was pushed in the back."

"It must have been Tom." I said, puzzled.

"It's pitch black; why is the door closed?" Fee's voice was quavering.

"This is probably Tom's idea of a joke." I said, feeling my way to the entrance. I shouted. "Come on Tom, the joke's gone far enough. You are scaring my sister. Open the door!"

There was no answer; the thick stone door stayed firmly closed. The silence in the tunnel was total, and it wasn't just darkness that surrounded us , but a terrifying blackness that you could almost feel.

"Ben, I'm scared."

"It's okay Sis, just hang on, the old fool will open the door in a minute. He's just trying to throw a scare into us."

"Well he's scaring me. I'm freezing cold and I can't stand this blackness much longer. For God's sake make him open the door, Ben, please." I could tell by the sob in her voice that Fee was near to breaking point.

"Tom, can you hear me? Open the door, please." No reply. The creepy feeling of unease that I had felt before about Tom was becoming magnified. What if he was some kind of psycho? You read about such people in the papers, you just never expect to meet one. With an arm around my trembling sister, we waited: There didn't seem to be anything else we could do.

"How long does he intend to keep us in here? I'm so cold Ben, and I'm scared." I could tell by Fee's voice that she was near to tears. And I didn't know what the hell to do.

"Don't worry Sis, I'll get us out of here." I said in desperation, trying to calm her down, and myself at the same time. Glancing at the luminous dial on my watch, I was shocked to find that we had been the tunnel for almost half an hour. This was no joke, was it? If it had been, Tom would have opened the door by now, surely.

"Oh what are we going to do Ben?" Sobbed Fiona.

"It's okay Fee, hang on, the old fool's got to let us out soon." Then a thought suddenly struck me. "Just a minute though. If this was originally an escape route for priests, surely there must be a way of opening the door from this side. Or they would be trapped, right?"

"I suppose so." Sniffed Fiona.

"Okay then, you feel around that wall." I turned her round to face the invisible stones. "And I'll take the other wall and the door."

"What am I looking for?"

Oh for Pete's sake, anything that sticks out, like that ring that Tom pulled to open the door from the other side."

In the pitch blackness we silently ran our hands over the damp, rough stones of the tunnel walls. Between us we must have covered every square inch of the walls near the door but found nothing but solid rock. The hope that had surged through us quickly turned to despair. Shivering with cold, we finally sank down on to the cold stone floor, huddling together for warmth. How long we stayed like this I don't know, but suddenly I leapt to my feet with a cry.

"What's the matter? What are you doing?" Came a scared voice from the dark.

"I must be stupid." I exclaimed. "What on earth are we doing sitting here?"

"How do you mean?" Said Fiona, mournfully. "What else can we do?"

"We can go along the tunnel, that's what we can do. If it leads to the church as Tom said, we can get out that way, right?"

"But it's pitch black, how will we find our way?"

"It's a tunnel, you dummy." I replied, a little more forcefully than I intended. There came a sniff from the darkness. "Sorry Fee, I didn't mean to snap. I'm just mad at myself for not thinking about it sooner." I gently helped my sister to her feet.

"Come on Sis, I'll go in front and you stick close behind me. We'll take it real slow in case there have been any roof falls or whatever. This would not be a good time to have an accident." It was a nerve wracking business, feeling our way along the tunnel; the blackness was so intense. I had the weird sensation that I was actually pushing it aside to make headway. I know one thing; I'll never see a blind person again without hurting for them. With my hands waving in front of me and my feet swishing about like mine detectors, progress was awfully slow.

"How much farther is it?" Whispered Fiona, like I was a tour guide or something.

"It can't be far now Sis, but remember we are going very slowly so just be patient, we'll get there." I must admit though, we seemed to have been shuffling along the tunnel for hours. I tried to recall how long it had taken us to reach the church this morning, but that didn't help much. Apart from the odd small rock, the floor of the tunnel was remarkably clear of obstacles considering how old it was. "Do you want to rest Fee?" I asked over my shoulder.

"Rest! Of course I don't want to rest. I just want out of here now." I smiled in the darkness. This was more like the old Fiona, all spit and vinegar. Then I stopped dead in my tracks, causing poor Fiona to blunder into the back of me. "Ow!" Yelped Fiona. "Why did you stop like that you idiot. You've made me bang my nose."

"Fee, I can see my hands, look!"

Chapter 15

I turned round to face my sister and sure enough I could just make out her blurred figure. No details, but it was not unrelieved blackness anymore. My spirits shot up like an express elevator.

"Come on Sis." I cried. "We are nearly at the end, look! We'll be out soon." Throwing caution to the wind, I grabbed Fiona's arm and began to move faster, almost dragging my sister along behind me. I could vaguely make out the walls and the floor of the tunnel now and with a cry of relief, could just discern the tunnels end, outlined by a soft yellow light. We stepped cautiously through an arch and into what was obviously the crypt of the church; with its grey stone walls and low vaulted roof. The crypt was lit by candles, set in small niches around the walls. Surprisingly though, the thick candles were dark green in colour instead of the usual white. Strange. However, I paid scant attention to that fact, I was more intent on finding a way out. And there it was, or rather wasn't. In a shadowy corner I could see a short flight of stone steps leading to... Nothing. The top of the steps ended in a blank, stone wall.

"Oh my sainted aunt!" I groaned, as I reached the top.
"Either somebody's walled up the entrance or it's another trick door."

"What are we going to do?" Wailed Fiona.

"Come on Sis." I urged, returning to the floor of the crypt. Don't give up now, there has to be another way out of here." And there was. In the opposite wall to the steps, half hidden behind a pillar, we saw an arched doorway, similar to the one we had just emerged from. The difference being that this tunnel was lit with the same green candles which illuminated the crypt. A thought suddenly struck me as I peered into the tunnel. "For Pete's sake! Who lit all these candles? And they must have been lit recently or they would have burned down, right?"

"Yes I suppose so." Murmured Fiona, gazing fearfully round the gloomy crypt, with it's shadowy cobwebbed corners, and awful forbidding silence.

"Of course!" I exclaimed, snapping my fingers. "Those monks must have lit them. The ones we saw this morning. I'll bet this is where they hold their services, or whatever it is that monks do."

"Then where are they?" Asked Fiona, reasonably.

"Well I don't know, do I? They probably went down this tunnel."

"Oh, did they?" Snorted Fiona. "Well they can jolly well stay there. I have had enough of tunnels for life."

"I'm sorry Sis, but we don't seem to have the choice. We can't just stay here, now can we? Anyway, this tunnel is different, it's lit. And nobody can shut us in because there's no door, right?"

Fiona just folded her arms and switched into her stubborn mode. It was time to play the masterful brother.

"You want to stay here by yourself then?"

My sister nearly choked. "Stay in this place all alone? You must be joking."

"Then come on, we have to find someone to help us get out of here, and this tunnel is the only way.

"Pig!" She muttered, but followed me through the archway into the tunnel. The same green candles cast a pale, shadowy light along the tunnel as we moved further in. I don't know what it was about those candles, but they gave me a rather uneasy feeling.

After a few yards, the tunnel bent sharply to the left and once again we could make out the arch at the end. But this time it was framed in a flickering, reddish glow. I took Fiona's hand and walking cautiously to the tunnel's end, we edged nervously through the arch.

"Welcome, we have been waiting for you."

Chapter 16

Fiona clutched my arm as we stared in disbelief at the incredible scene before us. The tunnel opened into what appeared to be a large, natural cavern, illuminated by the same green candles lit the crypt. However, here they were helped by several glowing braziers, which accounted for the red glow we had seen at the tunnels end.

The man who had spoken was dressed in a monk's habit, similar to the ones we had seen this morning. The cloth though, was not black as we thought, but a very dark green. The cowl threw his face into deep shadow; giving him an air of menace as he beckoned us silently forward. However, Fiona and I stood routed to the spot as we took in the incredible scene before us. Nothing could have prepared us for this macabre tableau. In the centre of the cavern was a huge block of polished stone, standing about four feet high. The top of it was so finely burnished that the object standing upon it, looked like it was floating on water. It was this object that rendered us incapable of moving. The monstrosity crouching atop the great stone was enough to strike terror into the bravest heart. If it hadn't been for Fiona, clinging to me like a limpet, I'm pretty sure I would have run; anywhere not to have to look at that obscenity ever again. Fiona gasped and I could feel her trembling with fear.

"Oh God! Ben, what is it?" What indeed; the huge stone horror which glared down from the raised dias was like a creature from the pits of hell itself. Hideously gross, it squatted like a huge toad, dominating the cavern. However, this monstrous thing was like no toad on God's green earth. From it's head protruded two forward pointing horns and three toed webbed feet were surmounted by terrible curved claws. Curling like an arch over it's back was a long forked tail. But all of these things were nothing compared to the thing's face. Though grotesquely toad like it was a shudder-some parody of a human face, with viscous fangs protruding from it's long slit of a mouth. The large red stones which were the eyes, caught the flickering light from the glowing braziers and seemed horribly alive, as they glared down upon the cowled figures kneeling below. The sculptor who had carved this repulsive, evil thing, though obviously brilliant, must have been barking mad.

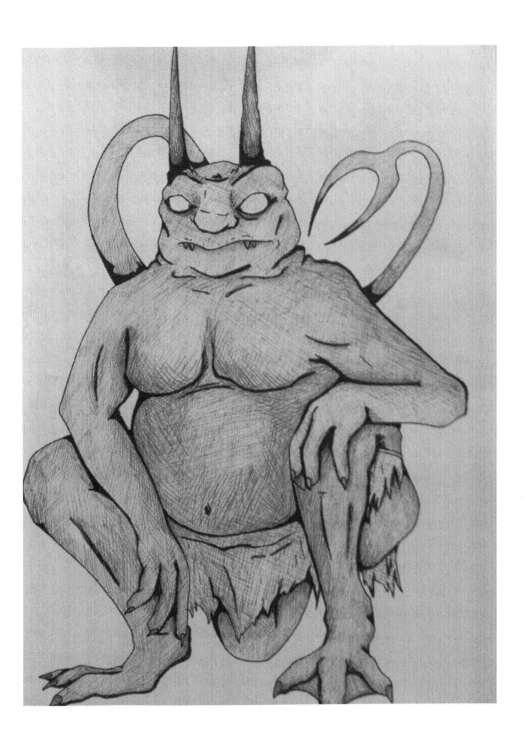

Chapter 17

The monk gestured again for us to move further into the cavern. "Come" he said, impatiently. "Time is short." Oh, is it, I thought. Well I was getting a real bad feeling about this place. Maybe they were just a bunch of harmless cranks; but then again maybe they weren't. Deciding it was time to put some distance between us and this pack of lunatics, I grabbed Fiona, and spun round. "Come on Fee, lets get out of here." I yelled, pulling her after me. However, we didn't get very far. Two of the monks had slipped silently behind us, cutting off our retreat back into the tunnel. Not that there was much chance of escape that way from what we had seen. We seemed to be caught like rats in a trap.

"Tie them." Ordered the first monk curtly. Fiona cried out in terror. "Ben! Ben! What are they doing? Stop them!"

"What's going on? What have we done?" I yelled, struggling to break free from the man holding me.

"Keep still and be quiet and you won't get hurt." He snarled, pulling my arms roughly behind me and tying my wrists together. A sobbing Fiona was being treated in a similar fashion.

Thrusting us in front of him, the first monk marched us behind the kneeling figures, to the back of the cavern. "Sit there and don't move." He snapped and then proceeded to tie our ankles.

"Now then, stay put. Do you hear?" He muttered hoarsely. I had another try.

"Why have you tied us up? What are you going to do with us?" Without replying, the man turned his back and moved silently away.

Poor Fee was scared to death and still sobbing, quietly. I shuffled closer to her. "Don't cry Sis, I'll get us out of this." It sounded hollow, even to me.

Suddenly, as one man, the monks rose slowly to their feet. One detached himself from the group, walked over to a shadowy alcove and sat down on a stool. I could just make out the pipes of an organ rising above him. So this was the source of that weird music that we had heard. The man raised his hands in the manner of a concert pianist beginning a recital. However, that's where the similarity ended. He brought them crashing down savagely onto the keys. A terrible dischord filled the cavern, causing Fiona and I to flinch as if from a blow. Then the chanting began. It was an awful sound. There was a kind of rhythm but nothing resembling a melody. It was as if it was being played and sung backwards. We both had an overwhelming urge to cover our ears to shut out the terrible dischordant noise. But since we were trussed up like a couple of turkeys we just had to suffer it.

Mercifully it finally ended and one of the monks left the others and moved out in front to stand beneath the great stone beast, facing the group. There was something familiar about this man. I couldn't see his face, it was thrown into deep shadow by his cowl. Maybe it was the way he carried himself, or his stance. But there was something. Turning to face the terrible stone beast, he threw up his arms and cried. "Bring them forward." Then I knew with a sickening certainty who was hidden beneath the green robe.

Chapter 18

John Warton, lay back in the comfortable armchair and stretched his feet towards the cheerfully glowing log fire. "I know it isn't what we were expecting love, but we could have fared a lot worse. The place is warm and cosy and the food is not bad either. I'll admit that the company could be a bit more congenial but you can't have everything."

"Mmm" murmured Elizabeth, his wife, who was only half listening as she held back the heavy curtain, peering into the swirling mist. "I wonder where the children are?" She mused.

"Well they are hardly likely to be out there, are they?" chuckled John.

"No of course not, but it's not like them to be late for meals, is it? They are usually looking for a snack to keep them going long before this." Elizabeth Warton, glanced at the slim gold watch on her wrist, letting the curtain fall back against the tendrils of the mist clawing at the window. "They surely aren't still playing table tennis."

"Oh stop worrying Liz, they'll turn up." Replied her husband with a chuckle. "They have never missed a meal yet as far as I know."

"Well, all the same I think I'll go and see if I can find them."

"Oh alright love, I'll come with you. It's about time I stirred myself I suppose." John Warton hauled himself, reluctantly, from his comfy armchair and followed his wife from the room. Climbing the wide staircase they made their way first to the games room. The place was in darkness and quite obviously empty.

"Let's try the bar." Said Elizabeth, turning towards the stairs.

"Yes" agreed John, "I'll bet they're stuffing themselves with Coca Cola and crisps." The bar, however, was deserted. Not only were the children not there; nobody else was either. John Warton rubbed his chin and gazed around, a puzzled expression on his face.

"What's the matter, Dear?" Asked Elizabeth.

"There's something strange going on here."

"How do you mean?"

"Have you ever been in a hotel where the bar was empty a few minutes before dinner?"

"Well since you mention it, no I haven't." Replied his wife, frowning.

"Nor have I." John Warton, walked purposefully to the bar and rang the quaint old hand bell, calling out at the same time.

"Tom, Molly, anyone there?"

Reluctantly, it seemed, Tom emerged from the room behind the bar. "Sorry, I didn't know anybody was in here." He muttered. John Warton glanced pointedly at his watch. "Wouldn't you expect guests to be in the bar for a pre-dinner drink around about now?"

"Ah" replied Tom, looking like a cornered rabbit.

"Anyway, never mind about that now." Snapped John. "Have you seen the kids anywhere?"

"No I ain't." Said Tom, a little too quickly.

"Are you sure?" John, had the strange feeling that Tom was hiding something.

"Course I am." Blustered Tom. "I'd know wouldn't I?"

"Come on Liz, we are wasting our time. We'll search this place from top to bottom. They must be somewhere." As they left the bar they bumped into Molly. "Ah Molly, we can't seem to find the children. Have you seen them anywhere?" Molly looked white and scared.

"No, no I haven't. Perhaps they went for another walk" she said, desperately. John glared at her, angrily. "For goodness sake woman, It's pitch black and the mist is as thick ever. They are not stupid."

"N-no Sir." Stuttered Molly, who looked as if she wished that she was anywhere but standing in front of an angry John Warton. "I have to go Sir." Said Molly, almost running down the hall.

John and Elizabeth Warton looked at each other with deep concern. "What on earth is going on in this place, John?" Her lips trembled. "Where are our children?" John Warton, put a comforting arm round his wife's shoulders. "Don't worry love, we'll find them. Look, the first thing we'll do is search this place from top to bottom." And search they did. Opening any doors that were not locked and banging on the one's that were, creating enough noise to wake the dead. "This is weird." Said John, "Apart from Tom and Molly the place seemed completely empty. Where on earth are all the guests? They were here this morning."

"Oh John! Something terrible has happened, I know it has."

"I'm going to call the police." Said John Warton, firmly. "This has gone far enough. But before I do, we'll take a look outside. I have a high powered lantern torch in the boot of the car." After quickly donning coats and scarves, John and Liz Warton stepped out into the clammy mist and made their car. John, took the big lantern torch out of the boot and turned on the powerful light. The beam lanced into the mist and the two worried parents walked around the inn waving the light and calling out the children's names.

"Ben, Fiona, call out if you can hear us and follow the light." Keeping within sight of the inn they walked all round it, calling out all the time. But all that came back was the mocking sound of their own voices which seemed to echo back from the mist.

Returning to the inn, John Warton, sat his wife down near the fire in the bar and called loudly for Tom. When the man arrived he looked shiftier than ever. "I still ain't seen them" He said defensively.

"Never mind about that." Snapped John. "Give me two whiskies and pass me the telephone." Tom blinked several times and licked his dry lips. "Come on man, you must have one behind the bar there."

"Oh we got one alright, but it's out of order."

"I don't believe you." John Warton, leaned over the bar, located the phone and hauled it towards him.

"Hey you can't do that." Cried Tom, reaching out. John knocked his arm away and lifted the receiver. There was an immediate purring of the dialing tone. "Out of order is it?" He glared at the barman. "I don't know what your game is or what's going on at this place. But just don't get in my way if you want to stay in one piece." John Warton rang the operator, who put him through to the police station at Princetown.

Chapter 19

Police constable Parry, who took the call, was at the tail end of a long shift and faced with a tedious journey home in the mist. "Princetown police." The unmistakable Devon burr came down the line. "Can I help you?"

"I certainly hope so." Replied John Warton, sharply. "My two children are missing."

"Just a minute sir." Said the constable, reaching into a draw for the appropriate form. "Let me get down some details. Your name is – –?"

"Warton, John Warton."

"Right Sir, could you give me the names of the missing children, and a description please?" John Warton, gave him the details, impatiently drumming his fingers on the bar. Elizabeth Warton, stood near her husband, white faced, her eyes clouded with worry.

"Right Sir, got that. Now when did you last see them?"

"Just after lunch, around two thirty." John, replied.

"You mean today?" P.C.Parry sounded surprised.

"Of course I mean today, man."

"But it's only seven thirty now, Sir. Don't you think you're jumping the gun a bit. You know what kids that age are like.

They will probably show up any time now." Constable Parry, waited hopefully, his eyes straying to the clock on the wall. Another 10 minutes and it would be Dave Collis's problem. "No," roared John. "I don't think I'm jumping the gun, as you put it. We have searched the inn from top to bottom. And even outside as far as we could in this blasted mist."

Constable Parry, sighed resignedly. "Whereabouts are you Sir?"

"We're staying at The Lost Inn. It's near a village called Boxwood do you know it?"

"Yes Sir, I know where Boxwood is. What about the other guests? Have you checked with them? They may have seen your children."

"That's another strange thing." Said John. "The other guests are nowhere to be seen. There's nobody in the bar or the dining room, and they are certainly not in their rooms. We have checked every room in the place."

Constable Parry, placed his hand over the mouthpiece and groaned. "Oh Lord, I've got a nutter on the line. He'll be on about aliens next. I'll bet a fiver on it."

"What are you on about Parry?" Asked Detective Sergeant Norris, without much interest. He was staring through the window at the unwelcoming night, and considering whether to book a room at The Black Bull here in Princetown. Rather than face the slow crawl home across the mist shrouded moor. The wife would moan, of course when he phoned. Still, it wasn't a bad idea.

"I've got a chap on the line who reckons his two kids are missing. Not only that though, he claims that all the other guests at the inn have also disappeared. I tell you, he'll be on about little green men any time now."

"Where is he calling from?" Asked D.S.Norris, still trying to make up his mind whether to go home or stay in Princetown.

"The Lost Inn over Boxwood way." The Detective Sergeant's head snapped round, his problem forgotten.

"Give me that phone." He snapped, striding over to the desk. The surprised P.C.handed over the receiver.

"Hello Sir, D.S. Norris here. Would you mind telling me what you have just told constable Parry. Sorry to make you go over it again but give me as much detail as you can please."

So John Warton, recounted exactly what had happened and how they came to be at the inn in the first place. When John, had finished, Norris, said "Alright sir, I'll be with you as soon as I can. But in this weather it may take some time. In the meantime, just stay put and try not to worry. Whatever you do don't go searching outside in the mist." He almost added, you are too close to the 'Great Pencarron

Bog', but stopped himself in time. No point in adding to their worries.

"You are not going over to Boxwood on a night like this on the word of some crank, surely Sarge" said the constable, appalled.

"Yes, Constable Parry, and so are you"

"But my shift finishes in 10 minutes, Sarge"

"Not any more it don't". Said D.S.Norris, firmly. "Who's due on?"

"Dave Collis" replied Parry, mournfully. "Good, he can come as well. You go and organise some big torches and bring some spare batteries. I'm going in to see the Guv"

D.S.Norris turned and walked towards a glass panelled door which bore the name, Detective Inspector Bromhill. Tapping on the glass has he walked in. "Excuse me Guv, just had a call from a chap who reckons his two kids have gone missing. Says all the other guests at the inn seem to have disappeared as well."

"A weirdo?" Queried the D.I." that's what I thought at first. But he was calling from The Lost Inn over at Boxwood. Ring any bells, Guv?" Detective Inspector Bronhill, put down the reports he had been scanning and his eyes narrowed. "Oh, yes" he nodded, thoughtfully. "Must be three years ago, if I remember correctly."

"That's right" said Norris, grimly. "Two young girls about 16 from around the village, disappeared without a trace."

"Go and pull the file on that case." Said Bromhill. When D.S.Norris returned with the file, the two men skimmed through the few pages together. "Same time of the year and similar weather conditions" mused Bromhill. "And a witness says he thinks he saw one of the girls walking near the inn on that day but couldn't be sure because of the mist. It was thought at first that the two girls had run away together. Headed for the bright lights, as it were. Then a scarf belonging to one of them was found a few days later on the edge of the Great Bog. With no evidence of foul play, conclusions were drawn and subject to any fresh evidence turning up, the case was closed."

"All a bit vague though, isn't it Guv?"

"Yes I agree, but they wouldn't be the first victims that vile Bog has claimed over the years. Not by any means."

"There's another thing that I was never happy about." Said Detective Sergeant Norris, tapping a page with his forefinger. Bromhill, leaned forward and peered at the page in question.

"Your interview with this Quentin Adams, you mean?" The sergeant, nodded. "But we had nothing on him, did we? I know he had this bunch of so-called monks, but we couldn't arrest him for that, could we." He gave a wry smile "religious freedom and all that, eh!"

"There was nothing remotely religious about Quentin Adams, Guv. Believe me. You don't meet many people that are truly evil but he is one." Detective Inspector Bronhill, nodded. "Anyway you had better be getting over there. That's if you can make it in this filth."

"Right Guv, I'm taking Parry, and Collis, if that's okay?"

"Yes of course. I'll get Karen, from upstairs to cover the desk. Just keep me posted."

Chapter 20

The journey from Princetown to Boxwood, was a nerve wracking business. Despite the battery of lights on the police Range Rover, the writhing mist fought back like some legendary monster, as if trying to wrap the car and its occupants in a clammy embrace.

"Curse this damned mist." Muttered D.S.Norris, his face taught and his eyes straining to penetrate the evershifting curtain in front of him.

"It can't be far to the turn off now Sarge" said Constable Collis, who was sitting in the front with Norris. "We just passed the road to 'Dumblehayes farm'. The Boxwood Road must be about two hundred yards on the right."

"Okay." Replied the Sergeant. "But keep your eyes peeled, and you in the back there, Parry, stick your head out of the window and yell if you spot the turning."

"Will do Sarge." Said P.C.Parry, as the window slid down. The dank chill swirled into the car like an invading army. The 200 yards stretch of road seemed to go on forever, until D.S.Norris was sure that they had missed it altogether, when Parry called out. "There it is Sarge, that's the signpost, we are right on it."

"Got it" said Norris, as he wrenched the wheel over into the narrow road that led to Boxwood and to The Lost Inn. it was another 20 tedious minutes before Norris, finally spotted the old stone pillars that stood like sentinels at the mouth of the drive. With a sigh of relief he entered the drive. "Hallelujah, we made it."

The lights of the inn, when they at last glimpsed them through the mist, were a welcome sight to the police officers. D.S.Norris passed the moisture covered cars and pulled up in front of the door, switched off the engine and killed the lights.

"This had better be on the level." Muttered Norris. "Or I swear I'll have somebody for wasting police time."

John, and Elizabeth Warton, who had seen the car's lights appear through the mist, were waiting anxiously in the hall. The D.S.introduced himself and two constables, and John led the way into the bar. "Still no sign of the children, Sir?" Asked Norris. John Warton, shook his head. "No, we have looked everywhere."

"This place is like a morgue Sarge." Observed Constable Parry, gazing round the room. Norris gave him a glare. "Right you two." He said. "I want this place searched from top to bottom, and I mean that literally. Start in the attics and finish in the cellars and don't miss anything in between.

If you find anybody, staff or guests, bring them to me, right?"

"Okay Sarge." And the two constables hurried away to search the inn.

"The cellars." Exclaimed John, "I completely forgot about the cellars"

"Just leave it to the officers, Mr Warton." Said Norris. "Let's be absolutely sure that your son and daughter are not in any part of the inn before we start searching out there." He nodded grimly towards the heavily curtained window. "Now where are the staff? Don't tell me they have disappeared as well."

"They were around a while back." Replied John. "As I said on the phone there seems to be just two of them. I'll see if I can raise them." Said John, walking to the bar. "Tom. Molly." he called. There was no reply.

"This is getting odder by the minute." said the detective, rubbing his chin. So there were other guests here when you arrived?"

"Oh yes." Replied John. "At least fifteen, maybe more."

"And they were all men." Put in Elizabeth. "Which I thought rather strange, didn't you John?"

"Yes" continued her husband. "I sort of got the feeling that they were together, you know, some kind of club or something. Weird bunch, I know that."

"Did you talk to any of them?" Asked Norris.

"Talk to them." Snorted John. "We didn't even get a 'good evening' when we came in. You would've thought that we had just arrived from Mars."

"We did speak to one of them, you remember." Said Elizabeth

"Oh yes, briefly. He told us some cockeyed legend about a band of smugglers getting swallowed up in the Pencarron Bog."

"Oh this moor is full of legends and folktales." Said Norris, dismissively. "Well, he was the only one who spoke to us. Strange man." Mused John. "Adams, I think his name was." P.S. Norris's head snapped up, without knowing. "Not Quentin Adams by any chance?"

"Why yes it was. Why, do you know him?" The Sergeant nodded grimly. "We have met." And uneasy feeling crept over him as if the mist had followed him inside.

Suddenly the door of the bar opened and Tom and Molly were propelled inside the room by Constable Parry

"Look who I caught trying to sneak out the back way, with their bags packed."

"Tom and Molly." Exclaimed John, in surprise. "I take it that these two are the staff?" Said D.S Norris. "Right just sit down there." He pointed to the table where John and

Elizabeth, were sitting. To Constable Parry, he said "Where is Collis?"

"He went down to search the cellar, Sarge."

"Go and give him a hand, I've got some questions for these two." Norris glared at the ashen faced pair at the table…

Tom tried to bluster, "Ere' you can't stop us from leaving if we want to go. We aint' done nothing and we don't know nothing."

"Nothing about what?" Snapped D.S Norris, leaning across the table. "Come on, I want some answers. Where are Mr Warton's children? And where are all the other guests?"

Molly, her eyes darting nervously at Tom, looked as if she was about to speak. But Tom glared at her and she remained silent. "We aint' got nothing to say cos we don't know nothing, honest." whined Tom. "Now can we go? You aint' got no right to keep us here." At that moment the two constables entered the bar.

"We've checked the cellar Sarge; It's deserted like the rest of the place. However, we did find this." P.C Collis reached out and placed a tiny gold elephant on the table in front of D.S Norris.

"That belongs to Fiona!" Cried Elizabeth, jumping to her feet.

"Are you sure?" Asked Norris, picking up the elephant and handing it to her.

"Oh yes, quite sure." replied Elizabeth, firmly. "It's off her charm bracelet. She collects animal charms and I recognise that one."

"What on earth was it doing down in the cellar?" John Warton was now also on his feet. D.S Norris, held up his hands. "Calm down Sir, we'll get to the truth, I promise you." To Tom, "Well, what have you got to say now?" The tiny gold charm glinted in the light as he held it up. "How did this get in the cellar?" His voice was deceptively soft but laden with menace.

"How do I know? yelled Tom. "It's got nothing to do with me." Then Molly, burst into tears, and in a stricken voice, said. "For God's sake, tell them or I will. It's gone too far now." Before Tom could utter a word, Norris thrust his face within inches of Tom's.

"You keep quiet, I'll hear this from Molly. So button it, right." Turning to Molly, the D.S said in a softer tone. "Alright love, let's have the full story. The truth now and don't leave anything out."

"It was him that made Tom do it." Sniffed Molly.

"Who made him do what?" coaxed Norris.

"Adams, that Quentin Adams. He aint' a nice man Sir." Molly's eyes darted wildly around as if expecting Adams to appear at any second.

Chapter 21

The eyes of the detective sergeant bored into Molly's. "Come on love, let's have it all. Nobody's going to hurt you; the truth now." Licking her dry lips and glancing nervously at the now silent Tom, she said. "He forced Tom to lure the children down into the cellar and show them the tunnel. " Norris looked questioningly at Collis and Parry. Collis shrugged. "We searched every inch of that cellar, Sarge. There was no sign of a tunnel."

"Course there wasn't" muttered Tom. "It's secret, aint' it."

"Where does it lead?" Demanded Norris, sharply.

"It goes down to the crypt of the old church, and then on to their secret temple. But I aint' never been in there." Replied Tom. D.S Norris, rose and pulled Tom to his feet. "Right, lead on and show us the tunnel."

"If I do will you let us go? whined the barman. "Just do it" snarled Norris.

"But why has he taken our children?" Cried Elizabeth. "What for?" her voice was scared and trembling. "It's for some secret ceremony." Said Molly. "They do it every year about this time. I'm sure they don't mean the children no harm." Norris looked grim, remembering the two village girls who went missing two years ago.

Chapter 22

After untying our legs, one of the monks lead us forward to stand in front of Quentin Adams; for that was who stared down at us from beneath the dark green cowl. Turning to face the awesome statue, Adams raised his arms towards the monstrous thing whose ruby red eyes seemed to be alive as they glowered malevolently down on the scene below.

"Oh glorious one, behold the offering we bring you this night. With these fey siblings, we the brotherhood summon you from your eternity of darkness beneath the great bog of Pencarron to share with us, your disciples, the awesome power of the sub world, of which you are the true lord. Reward our patience, oh great one and let there be a raising this night. Grant us the sight of your illustrious form." Quentin Adams' voice rose to a shout. "Asteroth, Asteroth!" The cry was taken up by the assembled monks, who also raised their arms as they cried the dreaded name aloud. Fiona, and I, stood helpless before Quentin Adams, and the toad creature which gazed down on us with evil red eyes. I don't know who scared me the most, Adams, who was obviously insane or the grotesque thing to which he was praying. Poor Fee, stood wide-eyed, and dumb with terror and I could do nothing to help her. Scared as I was, with my hands tied behind me, I couldn't even give her a hug to comfort her. "Chin-up Sis," I muttered quietly. "Mum and dad, will have missed us by now and they'll be searching. You can bet on that. They'll find us. Trust me."

Fiona, turned her head towards me and I could see in her eyes that she didn't really believe me.

Then a hush fell over the assembled company as Quentin Adams, slowly turned his face to his followers. "Come my brethren, the hour is upon us. The time of the raising draws nigh."

Adams picked up a torch from the pile and lighting it from one of the glowing braziers, turned towards an opening at the far side of the cavern. The other monks followed suit and the flaming procession filed solemnly through the arched doorway. Fiona, and I were prevented from escaping, by a length of rope slipped through our arms and held by the monk who seemed to be our jailer. Prodding us forward he followed in the wake of the others. Unlike the other tunnels through which we had come, this one seemed to be natural in origin. The rock walls varied in height and width and it twisted and turned this way and that. After what seemed in age, the tunnel ended in a blank wall; which was in fact a cleverly constructed door. The mechanism for opening it was similar to the one in the cellar. Quentin Adams, reached up and pulled some hidden lever and with hardly a sound, the door Swung outwards. Thick, grey mist swirled in at once, wrapping us in it's chilly embrace. Fiona and I began to shiver with cold. Unlike our captors in their heavy robes and cowls, we were dressed for indoors, not Dartmoor in the dead of winter. Not that any of them seemed very bothered about our welfare. After trudging through the mist for what I judged to be about another fifteen minutes, the column halted and the monks spread out and began ramming the long torches into the soft earth. When they had finished, the flaming torches formed a large semi-circle of light. In the centre stood Quentin Adams, and my sister and I were led out to stand before him. Although our feet didn't actually sink in, there was an ominously squashy feel to the ground on which stood. Then with heart stopping certainty I realised that we were on the edge of The Great Pencarron Bog.

Chapter 23

With D.S Norris, close behind him, a sullen Tom, led the way down into the cellar. Followed closely by John and Elizabeth Warton, Molly, and the two policeman bringing up the rear. Switching on the dim cellar lights, Tom walked the length of the cellar to the blank stone wall at the end. Norris, peered closely at the wall, looking for some sign of a door.

"If this is some sort of wild goose chase, you are going to be one sorry b----." Tom, sneered and reached for the rusty ring.

"Wouldn't be much of a secret door if you could spot it that easy, would it?"

"Just open the damn thing." Growled Norris. With everyone looking on expectantly, Tom pulled on the ring. However nothing happened, the door remained stubbornly closed. He tried a second time but with no result.

"Come on, come on!" Urged Norris. "Get the thing open."

"I'm trying, but it just won't open. It must be jammed." Gasped Tom, tugging at the ring.

"Here let me." Snapped the Sergeant, pushing Tom to one side. "If you are getting tricksy with me you'll wish you'd never been born." But despite Norris' best efforts the door would not budge. "For God's sake there must be another way in!" Cried John Warton in an anguished voice. "My kids are in there." Norris, glared at Tom, "Don't worry Mr Warton, we'll get to them even if I have to use his head as a battering ram."

"There is another way into the tunnels." Said a very scared looking Tom.

"Well where is it man?"

"There's a way in from the old church. It leads into the crypt. I only know that 'cause I heard them talking. Trouble is, I don't know where the door is, or how to open it."

"Come on we're not doing any good here." Said Norris. Leading the way out of the cellar, Norris called over his shoulder. "Parry, take care of these two and make sure they don't do a runner. And Collis, get the big lanterns from the car. We'll need all the light we can get." Back in the hall, Norris turned to John and Elizabeth Warton. "I should put on coats and gloves, it's pretty raw out there. And if you have torches, bring them along. Every little helps.

Despite the powerful police lanterns, progress was slow as they made their way along the gravel path. The chilling mist was as thick as ever as they passed through the lych gate and into the graveyard. It was an eerie journey along the path between the jumbled gravestones, half seen in the light of the lanterns. The old church loomed suddenly through the murk. Moisture glistening like tears on the rough grey stone.

Detective Sergeant Norris pushed open the heavy oak door and the rest of the party followed him in, looking nervously around. The unaccustomed light seemed to send the menacing shadows scuttling into corners like retreating phantoms. Norris and the two constables, swung the lanterns around as the group moved farther into the dusty old building.

"Where the devil do we start?" Said Norris, his voice echoing hollowly in the musty silence. Then to Tom. "Are you sure you don't know where the door to the crypt is?"

Before Tom, had time to answer, John Warton, spoke. "Well can we forget the walls. The crypt is usually under a church, right?"

"Good point." Agreed Norris. "So let's start checking the floor, starting at the far end." On the sergeant's instruction, the party began looking for - - - well, they didn't really know. Anything that could possibly be a secret door. It turned out to be a frustrating business for there were plenty of cracks between the centuries-old stone slabs of the floor. However no one found any rings or leavers or any other devices. After half an hour of fruitless searching, constable Collis, straightened up and groaned. "This is hopeless, Sarge. We don't even know what we are looking for." He said, leaning heavily against the old, carved wooden pulpit. "Hey" exclaimed Collis. "This thing moved. I'll swear it did." Everyone straightened up and moved eagerly over to where the old pulpit stood. Norris, and Collis, pushed and pulled but despite their combined efforts the large wooden pulpit, although seemingly loose, refused to budge. "Hang on." Gasped the sergeant. "Maybe there is a lever or a bolt somewhere. Let's get some light down near the base. See if there's anything that looks as if it might hold this thing in place." Everyone directed their lights onto the wide base of the old pulpit, while police officers and John Warton, examined the woodwork carefully; running the hand over the deeply carved wood.

After some minutes, Collis, gave an exclamation. "Look at this, Sarge!" The constable had discovered a loose panel that slid back to reveal a long, black bolt made of heavy, wrought iron. "This is more like it." Said Norris, his eyes gleaming with satisfaction. Without much tugging, the bolt slid easily from its socket. "Okay lads, try it now." Collis, and Parry, pushed on the large edifice, expecting resistance, but it swung easily round; revealing a large square hole. A flight of stone steps lead down into the blackness.

"Right." Said Norris, shining his light into the hole. "Let's see where this leads." Treading carefully, the detective sergeant, followed by the others, descended the short flight of steps.

Chapter 24

They found themselves in a short, narrow tunnel, which ended abruptly in a stone wall.

"Oh Lord!" exclaimed, Norris. "Not another trick door." However, Now they knew what to look for the search for the opening mechanism didn't take long. The ring was located in a hidden recess low down on the wall. "Got it!" Said the sergeant, triumphantly. "Stand back. I don't know which way this thing opens." At a tug on the ring, the end wall of the tunnel swung silently inwards; exposing another flight of steps leading down into the crypt.

"Well somebody has been here recently." Said Norris, indicating the candles flickering away in the recesses. "Green candles? Weird or what?" Observing the further tunnel, lit with the same green candles, Norris, held up his hand and in a low voice said. "Collis, you stay with me at the front. Parry, you take the rear. And everyone stay real quiet, okay?" They all nodded and Norris, led the way along the tunnel to the cavern entrance. Nearing the archway, the sergeant, signalled for them to stop. "Switch off the lights" he whispered. "I'll go and see what's ahead." Moving softly along the last ten yards to the archway, Norris pressed flat against the wall and peered into the dimly lit cavern. "Oh my god!" He gasped as his eyes rested on the grotesque idol, which looked even more sinister in the glow of the dying braziers. The party was silent; struck dumb by the stone horror which seemed to fill the cavern with an atmosphere of evil.

"Oh this is monstrous." Cried Elizabeth Warton, clapping her hands to her mouth. "Where are my children? What have they done with them?" John Warton, put a protective arm around his wife's shoulders. "Don't worry my love, we'll find them. I promise you."

Lighting up the cavern with the powerful police lanterns, they soon spotted the tunnel through which the monks had left. Detective Sergeant Norris, paused before entering the tunnel and turned. "You lads keep your sticks handy and when we find these lunatics, the first priority is to grab the kids. Any resistance, lay into them, okay? Never mind doing it by the book. Just get those children, understand?" The two police officers nodded. "Understood Sarge." Said Collis. "Right then, follow me."

Chapter 25

Following Norris, they wound their way through the twists and turns of the natural tunnel, until they were faced once more with a stone wall, with a sigh, the sergeant played his light over the old stones, until finally he found the lever which operated the door mechanism.

"Right, here goes." grunted Norris, pulling the lever towards him. This time a section of the wall swung outwards, letting in the dank chill of the moor.

"Ere' I don't like this." Muttered Tom, with a shiver.

"For once I agree with you." Said Norris, sniffing the mist laden air and frowning.

"What do you mean?" Asked John Warton.

"Can you smell anything?" John Warton took a breath and nodded. "Yes, there's a peculiar sour smell. What is it?"

"That" said Norris, grimly. "Is the unmistakable stench of the Great Pencarron Bog. And we are now on the edge of it." Directing his lantern down onto the ground, the sergeant grunted. "From the look of this turf, a lot of people went ahead from here. And if they can, so can we. But take it slow and keep in single file. This bog is not very forgiving. So for God's sake, don't wander off the track, okay?" There were murmurs of assent as the little party moved nervously

after the sergeant into the Pencarron Bog.

Chapter 26

At a signal from Adams, the monks began a monotonous chant; repeating over and over what appeared to be a name. "Asteroth, Asteroth." Out in front stood Quentin Adams, like some sort of high priest. With arms outstretched he carried on just as he had while standing before the stone beast in the cavern . As if trying to invoke this 'Asteroth' to appear. I tell you the fellow was seriously whacky.

The whole scene was like something from a horror film. Blazing torches in the swirling mist, the semi-circle of chanting monks. It almost made Fiona and I forget the damp and cold that seemed to have seeped into our very bones. Then the chanting suddenly ceased and two of the monks walked forward to stand one each side of Adams. The complete silence after all that chanting was nerve wracking. There was an air of hushed expectancy which hung over the Great Bog, for what seemed like an age.

I spoke softly to Fiona. "You okay Sis?" I asked. She nodded briefly. But I could tell that she was nearly at the end of her tether.

What happened next was everyone's worst nightmare. The stillness was broken by a kind of gurgling, slurping sound; which seemed to be coming from somewhere in front of us in the mist shrouded bog. Then, unbelievably, the slimy turf began to shiver and shake and to my amazement, started to heave upwards. But amazement soon turned to horror as suddenly the 'Great Bog' erupted in a massive fountain of slime. The sickening stench was beyond belief. It was as if a graveyard had given up it's dead. Then from the depths of the Great Pencarron Bog there rose a creature that surely must have come straight from Hell itself.

Everyone, including Quentin Adams and his monks, stood petrified as the gargantuan horror rose from its slimy lair.

Chapter 27

This was the obscene thing in the cavern, come to life, only twice as big and 10 times as terrifying. The creatures malevolent red eyes blazed down upon us and the huge squat body began swaying from side to side. From its jaws there came a hideous croaking roar which chilled the blood. From then on, to me, everything seemed to happen in slow motion. Quentin Adams, moved forward with raised arms, crying "master, master, you have come to us." The two monks on either side of him followed, reaching out as if trying to pull him back.

What happened next was to haunt my dreams for years to come. The beast reached out with its viscous, clawed forelegs and dragged Adams and his two companions into a deadly embrace.

Their screams as the monster dragged the three men further into the great, stinking morass were hardly human, but they were mercifully short. Then, as if waking from some awful spell, the monks turned and scattered into the mist. Except for one, thank God, who had the courage to dash forwards and cut the the cords binding our wrists. "Run!" He shouted. "Run for your lives". Then he turned and ran. I grabbed Fiona's arm and tried to run. But she just stood there like a sack of grain. The monster turned in direction the red eyes glaring balefully down.

"Fee," I yelled. "Come on, move." But she stood as if hypnotised by the loathsome creature in the bog. Desperate, I slapped my sister twice across the face, as hard as I could. Fiona, staggered back but at least she blinked and came out of the trancelike state. "Run Fee, run." I screamed, grabbing her hand and starting to run, pulling her, stumbling, after me. It wasn't a moment too soon, for as we turned the thing seemed to shriek with rage. Throwing a terrified glance back, I saw the great claws reaching for us and with a sickening dread I knew we were not going to make it. But there was no way I could leave my sister, who still couldn't coordinate her movements, despite my frantic pulling. I saw one chance to survive, and a slim one at that. The blazing torch that had been carried by Quentin Adams, was not in the semicircle with the others, but right in front of me. Letting go of Fiona, I pulled it from the ground, I swung the torch round and round and flung it as hard as I could at the grotesque beast that towered above us. I had no idea if it would work, but we just needed those few precious seconds to get clear. The monster let out a high-pitched scream as the fiery torch struck it squarely in the middle. "Come on Fee, please run, now."

Grabbing her hand again I jerked her forward and at last she seemed to realise what was happening and began to run with me across the soggy ground into the mist. Neither of us looked back, we just didn't dare.

I had no idea of direction. All that mattered was to get away from the awful apparition that Quentin Adams, had released from the depths of the Great Pencarron Bog for which he had paid the ultimate price. Now, however, we had a new enemy, the bog itself. The ground was becoming soggier every step, slowing progress to an exhausting plod. Our feet were now sinking up to the ankles and it was getting harder to pull them out. The Great Bog was sucking greedily as it seemed to sense fresh victims. This was truly an evil place. I look back over my shoulder into the mist, but there was no sign or sound of the monster, thank goodness. But Fiona, who was still trying desperately to forge ahead suddenly screamed. "Ben, Ben, Help me! I'm sinking!". I could just see her through the mist and struggled towards her. Already up to her waist she was thrashing about like mad. "Keep still Sis." I yelled. "Don't move. You'll make it worse, reach out to me, I'll try and get closer". But as I tried to reach my sister, my leg sank into the marshy ground right up to my knee. After struggling to get free I drew back. I'd be no use to Fiona if I joined her in the bog. There had to be something I could do. I couldn't just watch her get sucked down into that filth. Then I had a crazy idea, born of desperation. Taking off my denims, I called to Fee, who although she had ceased to struggle, was sobbing with despair as inch by inch she sank further into the bog. "Fee, listen to me." She slowly turned her head towards me, eyes filled with terror. "I'm going to use my jeans as a rope, so catch the leg when I throw it. Do you understand?" She nodded, dumbly. I leaned forward to get as close to her as

possible and keeping a firm grip in one leg of the jeans I tossed the other to my sister. She caught it like a drowning man clutches at a straw. But this was no straw, it was good, heavy denim. I pulled with all my might in this deadly tug of war. But The Great Pencarron Bog did not give up it's victims as easily as that. Despite my best efforts, I only managed to lift Fiona a couple of inches but at least I had stopped her sinking further for the time being. Now what? I was cold before but that was nothing to the way I now felt as I stood there in just shirt and underpants. I began to shiver uncontrollably, and Fiona, up to her waist in the icy slime of the bog, must have felt worse than I did. She was too cold now to even sob. And how long, I wondered, would it be before one or the other of us was too frozen to hold on any longer. I couldn't leave her to go for help, or she would sink. Not that I would have the slightest idea which which direction to go. More than likely end up in the bog myself. In desperation rather than hope, I began to yell for help while I still had enough strength. "Help, Help, for God's sake, help us!" I yelled at the top of my voice, over and over again. I don't know how long I had been standing there, supporting my sister, but with a start, I suddenly realised that I had been asleep. How anyone can go to sleep standing up to their ankles in a bog and holding on to the leg of a pair of jeans, I don't know. But I did. Perhaps it was the cold? I had heard stories of arctic explorers being lulled into sleep by the cold and never waking again. But for pete's sake, this was Dartmoor, not the North Pole. However, what had woken me was Fiona yelling my name. The leg of the jeans had fallen from my frozen fingers and Fee, had started to sink again. Grabbing the leg again, I hauled with all my strength, what was left of it.

"Oh Ben, what are we going to do?" Wailed Fiona. I was saved from trying to answer that question by a sudden bright light, which lit up our little tableau like a little stage set. It was the moon. Not a full moon, but to me it was like a search light. I gazed around in amazement, the mist had gone. Sure there were still a few wisps hanging around, but it was like magic.

"Fee, look! The mist has cleared, I can even see lights." Lights? What lights? They were some distance away but they looked like the beams of powerful torches. "Fee, yell with me, as loud as you can. I think it's a search party looking for us. We have got to make them hear us."

We both summoned what strength we had left, yelling and shouting until we just couldn't yell anymore. But the lights seemed to be moving away from us. They hadn't heard us. Oh, this wasn't fair, not after all we had been through. I gave one last shout, which sounded more like a croak and fell on my knees in the freezing mush. I had no strength left now, and my feet were dead. My fingers wouldn't bend enough to grip the end of the denim. Sobbing with frustration I leaned further over the bog and managed to wrap the leg of my jeans round my arm. I had to keep the tension or my sister would have no chance at all. How she was managing to hold on was a mystery. I had no idea how long all this had been going on, but I was now lying on my side. I don't remember going down but I felt so tired. Surely it wouldn't hurt if I just closed my eyes for a few minutes. But a voice inside my head said no. I had to hang on. Hang on to what? Oh God! The leg of the jeans. That snapped me awake and I tried to get to my feet, but I couldn't make it. However, I still had the leg wrapped round my arm, and it was still taut.

"Fee, are you okay?" I croaked. There was no answer.

"Fee, Fee, answer me please." I heard a faint moan and then to my horror the jeans went slack.

Chapter 28

What was I doing going up in a lift? And what were all the lights and voices? No, no I wasn't in a lift at all. I was in someone's arms being lifted from the ground. Suddenly I felt a surge of panic. "Fiona is in the bog and I've dropped the jeans. Oh God she'll go under." I began to struggle. "Take it easy son. Fiona's safe now. We have pulled her out, so just relax." The voice was Dad's, then I smelled a familiar perfume and Mum was stroking my face and crying. Wrapped in police tunics and Dad's coat, the men took in turns to carry Fiona, and I back to the inn. Even Tom took a hand, maybe his conscience was bothering him. On arrival at the inn it was hot baths and warm beds for Fiona and I. Followed by a visit from the police doctor, a plump, smiling lady in tweeds, whom D.S Norris had phoned, even before we had reached the inn. Although pale and scared looking, Fiona was recovering well. However, she insisted that she wasn't going to be left alone, so my bed was carried into her room by the two police constables. We had just settled in when Molly appeared with bowls of thick, rich soup and bread. Watching us devour our soup, Dad smiled.

"Ah the resilience of youth." He mused. "Considering the ordeal they have been through the seem in remarkably fine fettle, Liz" Mum nodded. "I'm just so thankful that we have them back."

"Well in that case" I said. "How about some more soup?"

"Some bacon and eggs would be nice." Added Fiona. Mum chuckled and rose to her feet. "I'll see what I can do. But it will probably be sandwiches. Okay."

After Mum left, there was a knock at the door and Detective Sergeant Norris entered. "Hello kids. Sorry about this Mr Warton, but I wonder if Ben and Fiona would be up to answering a couple of questions? I promise I won't keep them long. I can take full statements in the morning. "Dad looked at us and we nodded, the sergeant, smiled his thanks. "I would just like to know what happened to Quentin Adams and his cronies, if you feel up to telling me?"

I looked across at Fee, who shrugged, helplessly. It seemed that I was spokesperson. I was going to look a right idiot. But I had to tell the truth. Three men had died horribly out there in that terrible bog.

At that point, Mum entered with a tray of sandwiches and drinks. "Sorry, am I interrupting?" She said, putting the tray down on the dressing table. "No, it's okay ma'am, this won't take long, go on Ben."

I gave a sigh. "Well for a start, you are not going to believe this."

"Just take your time son." Said Norris, soothingly. I told the sergeant about the ceremony in the temple and how we had been taken by the monks, through the tunnel and into the Pencarron Bog. He was taking notes and nodding from time to time. Mum and Dad were sitting on our beds, listening intently. However, when I got to the part about the monster and the horrific fate of Adams, and his two fellow monks, their expressions changed. In Dad's case to the one he often uses on me. Where his eyebrows rise and he narrows his right eye and sighs. "Oh Ben!" exclaimed Mum, shaking her head in disbelief.

"Could you describe the monster you saw?" asked Norris, quietly. So ignoring Mum and Dad's incredulous faces, I described the thing that had reared up from the bog and taken the three men. I even told him about the foul smell. The sergeant's keen grey eyes bored into mine. But I held his gaze without flinching. I know what I saw. Then Dad said gently. "I think poor Ben, must have been delirious for a while back there. Which is not surprising after the terrible experience they have both endured in the last few hours. What you have just described, Ben, is that foul stone beast in their so called temple."

"Ben is telling the truth." Said Fiona, firmly. "I was there as well, remember."

D.S. Norris, stroked his jaw. "They could have been hypnotised, I suppose." He mused, thoughtfully. I looked across at my sister who simply shook her head, resignedly. "I told you at the start, you wouldn't believe me, didn't I. Well you don't, so that's it. I won't mention it again. I'd just as soon forget it anyway. Though I doubt if either of us ever will." Fiona, gave a shudder. "It's alright Ben." Put in Mum, soothingly. "Just relax and get some sleep. Things will look better in the morning." They always did to Mum, bless her. "Now leave the children to get some sleep, you two." She said, sheperding Dad and the police officer out of the room. "Just leave the light on Mum." Mumbled Fiona, drowsily. Amen to that, I thought. I had sure had enough of darkness for a while. We awoke next morning to sunshine sparkling on the frosty ground. Then a lot of things happened in a short space of time. Starting with Mum bringing in breakfast at about nine thirty. This was followed by another visit from the police doctor. After giving us a thorough going over, she snapped her bag shut, smiled and said "You have certainly got a couple of tough young cookies here, Mrs Warton." "You're sure they're alright?" Mum was a right worrier. "Right as rain. If all my patients were as healthy, I'd be out of a job." She chuckled. "Couple of weeks they will have forgotten all about Pencarron and it's bog." Fat chance, I thought.

Our next visitor was Detective Sergeant Norris, who took our formal statements in great detail and didn't even blink when we went over the part about the monster once again. I don't know if he believed us or not, but at least he appeared to take it seriously. After he had finished writing, we signed the statements and Dad, who had been sitting quietly, signed as well. Norris folded the statements and put them in his pocket. Rising to his feet he shook hands with Dad, threw us a smile and said. "Goodbye you two. Goodbye Mr Warton, have a good journey." He turned towards the door.

"We know what we saw, we weren't making it up, you know." I muttered, stubbornly.

Chapter 29

D.S Norris, who was about to leave, turned and regarded us seriously. "I'm not saying I believe or disbelieve you son. I have taken your statements and as far as I am concerned, that's it. I'll say this though, there are some very strange stories about The Great Pencarron Bog. They go back centuries, and yours is just another to add to the list."

"What happens now?" Asked Dad. "I noticed that the mini-bus which was parked in front of the inn has gone. I assume it belonged to Adams?"

"Yes, I checked the number plate with the station computer. They must have slipped past us in the mist, grabbed their belongings and made a run for it as the mist cleared."

"Road blocks." I suggested. Norris shrugged. "Oh we did that, son but they had a good hour start. They will have dumped the mini-bus as soon as they cleared the moor if they've any sense, and taken buses or trains out of the area. We'll fingerprint the van when we find it, and their rooms of course. However, if none of them has a criminal record, it won't help much. But we shall not stop looking, depend on it."

"What about Molly and Tom?" I asked. I felt rather sorry for Molly. Not Tom, though. They could throw the book at him as far as I was concerned. Norris, pursed his lips. "Well, they were both terrified of Adams, who apparently had some sort of hold over both of them. I don't think they'll be too hard on Molly but Tom will do time. After all, he played a major part in your abduction."

"So you won't need us anymore?" Dad asked.

"No sir, we may need to talk to you again if and when we make any arrests. But for now you are free to continue your journey. The Tregarron Arms, wasn't it? Nice place, I hear."

"Not as nice as the place we are going to" Said Mum, who had just entered the room. All eyes turned towards.

"What place is that then, Mrs Warton?" Asked Norris, looking puzzled. "It's a place called home." Answered Mum, with a smile. "What do you say kids?"

"Whoopee!" I yelled. Even Fiona, beamed with pleasure. Dad put his arm around Mum's shoulders and gave her a hug, a huge smile on his face. "Well, what are we waiting for?" he said. "Let's get packing."

"Hold it! Hold it!" I wailed. "What about Christmas dinner? There'll be no food in the house."

"They have supermarkets in Devon, you doughnut." Sneered Fiona.

"We'll pick up all we need on the way home, right Mum?"

"Right it is." Replied Mum, with a chuckle. "And don't call your brother a doughnut." Things sure were getting back to normal.

The police officers helped us carry our bags to the car, and with such Merry Christmassing and Happy New Yearing, we were off.

Fiona and I turned, and kneeling, looked out of the rear window at the centuries old Lost Inn. Off to the left we could just see the square top of the church. To the right lay The Great Pencarron Bog.

As the car rolled down the gravel drive we could see the beginning of that vast area of marsh. Despite the cloudless sky, the sunlight didn't seem to quite reach there. Or was it my imagination. We looked at each other, Fee and I turned, and slid down into our seats. The memories of that evil place were still too fresh. Dad turned onto the main road across the moor and headed north for home. Right now that word sounded wonderful to me. Half turning his head, Dad said, cheerfully "Okay kids, the first supermarket we come to, we'll buy everything we need for a slap up Christmas. What do you say?"

"Great" We chorused. Then Dad went and spoiled it. "And I promise you a real monster of a turkey."

You know, I wish he hadn't said that.

THE END

3226992R00065

Printed in Great Britain
by Amazon.co.uk, Ltd.,
Marston Gate.